Contents

The Golden Book of
FAIRY TALES

Translated by *Marie Ponsot*
Illustrated by *Adrienne Ségur*

A Golden Book • New York

Adrienne Ségur

The Sleeping Beauty

ONCE upon a time, there lived a brave king and his fair queen. For years they longed to have children, and at last the queen had a baby girl.

Her baptism was celebrated royally. All the fairies in the land (there were seven that year) were godmothers. This was a good, practical idea. Their gifts could make any baby perfect in every grace and virtue.

After the baptism, the king gave a party for the fairies. Seven places were set with big golden dishes that winked with diamonds and rubies. There were forks, knives, and spoons to match. As they sat down, in came an old, old fairy. No one had thought to invite her, for she had shut herself up in a tower fifty years before. Everyone thought she had died long ago or been enchanted.

A place was set for her at once, but with ordinary silverware. Only seven golden settings existed, for they had been made especially for the godmothers.

The old, old fairy muttered angrily, "Insult me, will they? They'll see."

A young fairy heard her, and feared mischief. So she waited to be the last to give the baby a gift, just in case the old one tried any tricks.

The youngest fairy gave the baby great beauty. The next gave her wit; the third gave her graciousness. The fourth and fifth made her an excellent dancer and singer. The sixth gave her skill with musical instruments.

Then it was the turn of the old, old fairy. Spitefully, she said, "The princess will cut her finger on a spindle, and die."

Everyone was shocked to tears. The seventh fairy stepped up, saying, "Fear not, your majesties. I can't undo this wicked wish completely. But I can change it. When the princess cuts her finger, she won't die. She'll sleep a hundred years, and be awakened one day by a king's son."

The king did what he could. He made a strict law forbidding spindles in his kingdom. But alas, the bad fairy's magic was too strong for him, as he was to find out.

One day, fifteen years later, the young princess decided to explore the castle. High in a tiny room, where nobody ever went, she saw an old woman, smiling and spinning, a distaff in her hand.

"Please, what's that?" asked the princess.

"A spindle, my dear," said the old woman, who hadn't heard of the fairy's curse.

"May I see?" the princess asked. As she reached out, she cut her finger on the spindle. She fell, unconscious, to the floor.

"Help!" called the old woman. All the king's servants came running. They tried frantically to revive the princess. They put cold linen to her head, ammonia to her nose, rose water on her wrists and brow. Nothing helped.

When the king saw her, he knew the curse had come true. He gave orders to the maids-in-waiting. Soon the Sleeping Beauty lay in her best dress, in a room all tapestried with gold and silver. The magic sleep increased her beauty. Her cheeks and lips were rosy. The soft sound of her breathing showed she wasn't dead, but sleeping.

The fairy who had saved her life was a thousand miles away on the fatal day. But a dwarf, who owned a pair of seven-league boots, sped off to tell her the bad news, and within an hour she arrived at the castle.

The king explained to the good fairy the arrangements he'd made for the sleeping girl. He asked, politely, for the fairy's opinion.

"The princess might be sad if she awakes in an empty castle," said the fairy. "I'll provide her with company and servants."

The king and queen watched as she put the household to sleep. Soon everyone slept: maids-in-waiting, chambermaids, serving maids, up-stairs maids, downstairs maids, maids of all work, cooks, potboys, houseboys, stableboys, valets and butlers, guards and gardeners, and all the animals in the royal stables. Even the princess's little dog, Poufle, was put to sleep at his mistress' side.

Then the king and queen kissed the princess, and went off to live in another palace. The fairy made a thicket of trees and thorny vines grow overnight around the castle. It was so dense that neither man nor beast could cross it. It was so high that nothing showed above it but the tops of the castle towers. Sleeping Beauty was in no danger from idle curiosity.

A hundred years passed. The king of that time had a son, who went hunting, one day, near the thicket. He saw the castle towers, and asked what they were. He got fifty different answers. One man said witches worked there. Another said it was alive with ghosts. Many thought it the home of a hungry ogre.

Then an old man said, "When I was a boy, my grandfather said that a princess slept in that castle. A fairy put her to sleep for a hundred years. Only a prince can awaken her."

The prince felt sure the old man was right. "What an adventure!" he thought. "I'm going to see for myself."

Thoughts of love and glory made him brave. He went toward the dense thicket. As he came near, the thorny tangles drew magically apart. He went ahead, alone, surprised to see the thicket close tight again behind him. Only he could pass through it.

Within the courtyard, all was silence. Men and animals lay everywhere, asleep. The prince went into the castle, passing through room after room of sleeping people. At last he came to a golden room, and there on a high bed was the fairest sight he'd ever seen. The sleeping princess was so lovely that even the sunlight seemed brighter where she lay.

Trembling, the prince knelt beside her. And, since the hundred years were up, the princess awoke. She looked at the prince as if she'd known him always.

"Is it you, my prince?" she whispered. "I've waited so long."

The prince's heart leapt for joy. He told her at once that he loved her absolutely.

Meanwhile, the other sleepers had wakened, too. Since they were not falling in love, they were all very hungry. The maid of honor announced, firmly, "Dinner is served."

The prince helped the princess to rise. He didn't say that her dress, though lovely, was very old-fashioned. In style or out, to him she was perfectly beautiful.

They dined well, while a quintet played music popular a hundred years before. The prince wasted no time. After dinner, the princess' chaplain married them in the castle chapel.

The next day, the prince went home. He told his family he'd lost his way, and spent the night in a logger's cabin. He kept his marriage secret from his mother. She was an ogress by birth, had a bad temper, and hated surprises.

At the end of two years, the prince and princess had two children. The elder was a girl, named Dawn. The second was a boy, and they called him Day.

Soon after Day's birth, the old king died and the prince became king. He announced his marriage, and brought home his little family with great ceremony.

The next summer, he had to go off to war. He asked his mother to rule in his place.

When he had left, his mother sent the young queen and her children to a country house in the woods. A few days later, she came to visit them.

She called the cook, and said, "I want little Dawn for dinner tomorrow."

"Oh, Your Majesty!" said the cook.

"Yes," said the queen, in the urgent voice a

hungry ogress has. "And mind you make a tasty sauce to go with her."

The poor man knew that there was no arguing with an ogress. He got his knife, and went to Dawn's room. The little girl ran up, laughing, and asked for a story. She was so sweet and merry, the cook couldn't bring himself to hurt her. He left her in peace.

In the barn, he chose a young lamb, and prepared it for the next day's dinner. Meanwhile, his wife hid Dawn in a hayloft. The ogress queen ate up all the lamb greedily, saying, "She's even tastier than I'd expected."

The next Sunday, she said to the cook, "I want little Day for lunch." He didn't protest, but hid Day with Dawn in the hayloft. Then he prepared a tender young goat for lunch.

The ogress sent him her compliments on his cookery.

So far, he had managed well. But then the ogress said, "Now I shall eat the queen. Make the same sauce you served with the children."

This was going to be difficult, the cook thought. The queen was over twenty, without counting her hundred years asleep. The farm animals were too young and tender to resemble her.

Fear for his own life made the cook decide to kill the queen. He went, armed, to her room. He was no sneak. Respectfully, he told her the instructions her mother-in-law had given.

"Do as you must," said the queen, tipping back her head. "I'll die gladly, and be with my eaten children again." She didn't know her children were safe.

Her bravery disarmed the cook. "No, my lady," he said. "I can't do it. You needn't die to see your children. I've hidden them safely, and I'll hide you, too. The old queen will eat a deer in your stead."

He hid her in the hayloft, and cooked a young

deer. The ogress ate every bit, very pleased. She planned to tell her son, when he should return, that wolves had devoured his family.

But one day, the ogress went strolling and happened to pass the hayloft. She heard children laughing, and a mother's voice hushing them. She recognized the voices. It was the young queen, with her children.

The ogress was furious to see she'd been tricked. She howled, "Get the biggest basin in the kingdom. Set it in the courtyard. Before tomorrow morning, fill it with snakes, vipers, toads, and a few spiders. The queen, the children, and the cook will be thrown into it to die. And I'll watch."

The next day, the ogress' servants made ready to throw the young queen into the squirmy, loathsome basin. Suddenly, the king rode through the gate, home unexpectedly from his wars.

"What on earth is going on here?" he demanded.

No one dared speak.

The furious ogress saw she couldn't always have her own way. So she jumped right into the basin, and was eaten up in an instant.

The king was upset for a while. But his distress gradually disappeared in the pleasure of being at home, with his beautiful wife and his two pretty children.

The Frog Princess

THERE WAS once a Tsar who had three excellent sons. One day the Tsarina, his wife, said to him, "Sire, our sons have grown up. They need wives."

The Tsar agreed. For a day and a night he thought hard. Then he sent for his sons, and said, "My sons, you must marry. Get your bows and arrows, and go to the castle gate. Shoot once, in any direction you like. Where the arrow falls you'll find your bride."

The princes obeyed. The eldest aimed to the right. His arrow sped over a wood and fell at the feet of a lord's daughter. She plucked it from the ground, and the prince came to claim her.

The second son aimed to the left. The arrow sped over the fields, and fell in a rich merchant's garden. The daughter of the merchant saw it strike among the roses, and picked it up. Soon the prince came, and claimed her as his bride.

The youngest son, Ivan, shot his arrow straight ahead. To find it again, he hunted two days and two nights. At last he came to the rim of a marsh. There, by the inky water, was a great green frog with gold-flecked eyes. In her mouth she held Ivan's arrow. A frog! How could he marry a frog? Poor Ivan ducked behind the tall reeds and tried to run off. But the frog had seen him. She croaked, "Frog though I may be, if you don't marry me, you'll regret it. Don't forget it!"

Ivan shuddered. He knew he must obey his

father. He bent over, picked up the frog, and carried her, dripping wet as she was, next to his heart.

When the brothers returned, the Tsar set a wedding day. The eldest son wed the noble lady. The next son wed the rich merchant's daughter. And Ivan wed his frog.

Some time later, the Tsar summoned his sons. He said, "Let's see what clever wives you have. Here are three pieces of cloth, all alike, one for each. Ask your wives to make me some shirts." He gave them his size and added that he wanted the shirts the very next day.

The eldest sons' wives called in all their maids and servants, and everybody began to snip and sew.

Ivan went to his frog wife. He was sad for her as he told her, "Father sends you this length of cloth. You are to make him a shirt during the night. He wants to know how well you sew."

"Believe in me, and you shall see," croaked the frog.

When her husband had gone, the frog chewed the cloth to bits and spat it out the window, saying, "Evening breeze, morning breeze, fair winds, come soon! Stitch me a royal shirt with the rays of the moon!"

Next morning, Ivan went to his wife's room. "Here you are," she croaked. "A shirt for the Tsar!"

Each prince gave the Tsar a shirt. The Tsar examined them with care.

To the eldest, he said, "This shirt I'll wear when I wash my dog."

To the next, he said, "It's a fair shirt. I'll wear it under my bathrobe."

To Ivan, he said, "A splendid shirt! A royal birthday, Christmas, Easter shirt! A shirt for special occasions!"

Soon the Tsar sent for his three sons again, saying, "I'm sure your wives do tapestry work.

But let's see who works best." He gave each son an equal amount of silks, colored wools, and gold and silver thread.

The two elder sons' wives called all their servants and set to work.

Sadly, Ivan explained to his wife what the Tsar wanted. "Believe in me, and you shall see," she croaked.

He left, and she tossed the gay heap of materials out the window, saying, "Evening breeze, silky breeze, silver moon and golden star! Weave, weave for me, please, my gift to the Tsar!"

The princes stood by as the Tsar inspected the three rugs. To the eldest, he said, "This might keep rain off a cow's back." To the next, he said, "It will do for a back-door mat." To Ivan, he said, "Lovely! I'll put it on my ivory table, for Sunday use only."

Next day, the Tsar said to his sons, "Princes' wives must bake royal bread. Here's the flour. See you tomorrow!"

This time the wives of the elder brothers tried to do whatever Ivan's frog did. All three mixed and kneaded the dough alike. But the frog whispered to her dough, "Rise light, and bake right. Be sun-gold and snow-white!" Then she put it in a cold oven.

The others had heated the ovens as usual. One loaf was burned black. The other was quite uncooked. The Tsar took the three loaves, and tasted each one. Of the first, he said, "A starving man might try to eat it." Of the second, he said, "Even rats wouldn't touch this gluey mess." Of the third, he said, "How light it is, and golden! I must give a dinner party, and share it with my guests."

Then he invited his sons to bring their wives to dine with him. Ivan, sure of disgrace for his poor frog, gave her the message.

On arrival the guests went to the reception

hall. Soon everyone was there but Ivan's wife. The elder sons' wives hoped she'd make the Tsar furious by failing to come. But then they heard the sounds of a great troop of horsemen, who surely must be escorting an important guest. "Who can it be?" exclaimed the Tsar.

At the window, Ivan replied with joy, "Father, it's my wife!" She entered, no frog, but a girl lovely as the dawn, royally robed.

During dinner the elder sons' envious wives copied every move Ivan's wife made. So when she put wine up her right sleeve and slid chicken bones up her left, they did the same.

After the feast was over, the Tsar asked the three girls to dance for him. Ivan's wife rose to obey. She shook her right sleeve, and a bright fountain sprang up on the floor. She shook her left sleeve, and two swans flew to the fountain pool.

The other wives followed suit. But they soaked their partners with wine, and hit them in the face with chicken bones. The Tsar crossly sent them home.

Meanwhile, Ivan had gone to his wife's room. On the bed he saw the frogskin. He picked it up and threw it on the fire.

Just then his princess rushed in, and cried, "What have you done? Now I must leave. And you'll have to cross a dozen dozen kingdoms to see me again. For I am Vassilissa the Wise!" With these words, she became a white swan and vanished into the blue.

Ivan bitterly regretted his impatience. His wife, frog or princess, had always been good to him. He should have loved her as she was. Somehow he'd find her, he swore. Off he set, on his finest horse. When the horse could go no more, Ivan tumbled off into the grass and slept. He awoke to see an old man, sitting on a rock and watching him.

The old man said, "Prince, good day. You talked strangely in your sleep—all about a frog fair as dawn. What's happened to you and what do you seek?"

Ivan told his story.

"Burning that frogskin was bad," nodded the old man. "It wasn't yours. It's bad to ruin other folks' things. And do you know whom you had the luck to love? Vassilissa is the Sea King's daughter! Her father punished her, after a family quarrel, by making her a frog for three years. If only you'd been patient! But I see you are sorry now. For that, I'll give you this ball. Roll it ahead of you. Go wherever it goes; never lose sight of it." Then the old man disappeared.

Ivan followed the ball for days, nights, weeks, over dozens of kingdoms. The journey was long; it was hard; but Ivan wanted so much to see Vassilissa that he kept on.

At last he came to the ocean's edge. There he saw a hut standing on chicken legs, turning, turning like a top. First it showed its front-with-a-door; then it showed its rear-with-a-window. Ivan cried, "Good hut! Turn your back to the sea! Stand and show your front door to me!"

The hut stood still. Ivan went in, and told his tale to an old crone at the fire. When he'd finished, she said, "You're in luck. Vassilissa is hidden in my sister's hut, secreted inside a bundle of twigs. Take that bundle, break it, and you shall see what you shall see!"

Afire with hope, Ivan sped off. Once he even got ahead of his ball. But he went back. Impatience had made enough trouble for him already. Finally he saw another hut on chicken legs, turning, turning like a top. First it showed its front-with-a-door; then it showed its rear-with-a-window. Ivan cried, "Good hut, if you will, please stand still!"

The hut stood still, and Ivan went in. An old

crone was tying a bundle of sticks with golden cords. Ivan knew that Vassilissa the Wise was hidden in the bundle. He waited until the old crone locked it away in a box. Then, quick as a flash, he seized the key, opened the box, took the bundle, and at one blow broke the bundle over his knee.

Vassilissa, pure as dawn and more lovely, appeared before him. She threw her arms round Ivan's neck and murmured, "Oh my prince! You have broken the spell. Now I'm your true wife for ever and ever!"

They returned to the Tsar's palace where they lived happily to the end of their days.

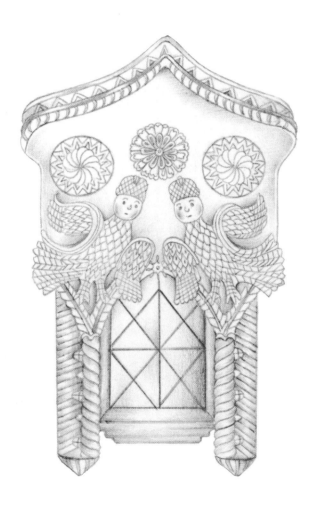

Donkey-Skin

ONCE upon a time, there was a lucky king. He was strong, noble, and wise. His subjects loved him. His neighbors respected him. His wife was fair and good; their love was deep and true. They had one daughter, so bright and dear that she was all the world to them.

Their palace was grand and comfortable; their courtiers were loyal, smart, and sensible; their servants liked hard work. Their huge stables housed the world's best horses. The marvel of the stables, however, was not a horse, but a donkey.

The king kept him in a luxurious stall, with a hundred servants all his own. The king had a good reason for this. For the donkey never simply soiled his bedding. Instead, each morning the bedding was found covered with heap upon heap of gold coins.

One day the queen fell ill. All the doctors in the kingdom couldn't cure her. She felt her end was near. She said to the king, "I have a last request. When you remarry . . ."

"Never!" interrupted the sad king.

The queen went on, calmly, "You must remarry. Your ministers will insist that you have sons to succeed you on the throne. Only promise me to wait until you find a wife better and fairer than I. Promise me this, and I'll die happy."

The king promised solemnly. And the queen died, happy in the knowledge that there were none to be found as beautiful as she. The king's ministers wanted him to remarry at once. He wept, told them of his vow, and defied them to find anyone as fair of face and as good of heart as his late queen. But the ministers insisted. At last the king promised to look around for a wife.

He visited all the families that had unwed princesses, but not one princess could compare with his late wife. Unhappily, he soon decided that the only princess fairer and better than his late wife was his own daughter.

He told his daughter that he would marry her, since she alone met with the conditions of his promise.

She begged and begged him, as well she might, to forget the idea. But he would not change his mind. The princess was frantic. That night she went, in a carriage drawn by a clever sheep, to see her godmother, the Lilac Fairy. The fairy comforted her, and told her what to do.

"To wed your father would be wrong," said the Fairy. "But you needn't refuse him outright. Instead, tell him to get you a dress the color of the weather, before you give him an answer. Rich though he is, he'll never find a weather-colored dress."

The princess thanked the fairy. Next day, she told her father that she would answer his proposal after he had given her a weather-colored dress.

The king summoned the finest dressmakers. "Make my daughter a weather-colored dress at once," he said. "If you fail, you'll hang."

The dressmakers soon delivered the dress. The sky itself was no lovelier, blue, cloud-soft, and shimmering. The princess didn't know what to do. She asked the Lilac Fairy.

"Demand a dress the color of the moon," said the fairy.

The king ordered a moon-colored dress from his best silversmiths. He was in such haste, they finished it the next day. It was a marvel of soft radiance. But the sight of it sent the princess to her room in tears.

The Lilac Fairy said, "Now, ask him for a dress the color of the sun. At least it will keep him busy until we think of a way out of this."

The king ordered the sun-colored dress. He even gave his rarest jewels to add to its brilliance. When it was done, it shone so like the sun that those who saw it were dazzled.

The princess went hopelessly to her room. The Lilac Fairy was very vexed by the king's success.

"Now," she said, "we must ask him something really hard. Demand the skin of his dear famous donkey, who gives him all his gold. Go ahead."

The princess did ask the king. He thought it a queer wish, but he did not hesitate. The donkey was killed, and its skin brought to the unhappy princess.

Her godmother found the poor princess weeping. "Don't cry, child," she said. "Misery can turn to joy if you're brave. Wrap up in the donkey-skin. Leave here, and walk until you can walk no more. If you give up everything for virtue's sake, heaven will reward you richly. Go. And take my wand. All your dresses will follow you underground, in this trunk. When you want them, tap twice with my wand. Now hurry."

Huddled in the ugly donkey-skin, and all smeared with soot to hide her beauty, the princess left the palace.

The king was wild to find her gone. He sent a hundred and ninety-nine soldiers and one thousand one hundred and ninety-nine policemen to find her, but they failed.

The princess went far, hunting for a place to stay. Now and then kind folk fed her. But she was so dirty they never let her stay. At last she found a big farm, where a girl was needed to empty the slops, clean out the pigsties, and do all the dirty jobs. The farmer thought that such a dirty girl would be just right for the job.

The princess was glad to agree. She worked hard among the fowl, sheep, and pigs. Soon, despite her filthy looks, she was known as a good worker. She was allowed to live in a tiny hut near the pigs.

One day, she passed a pool of clear water and saw her reflection. The dirt and the donkey-skin disgusted her. Quickly, she bathed, and saw herself beautiful once more. Of course, she had to hide in the donkey-skin again to return home.

But the next day was a holiday. Alone in her hut, she took the fairy wand, and summoned her trunk. Soon she was immaculate and splendid, jeweled and curled, in her weather-colored dress.

That same Sunday, the son of the king to whom the farm belonged went hunting. On the

Adrienne Ségur 1951

way home, the young prince stopped at the farm.

He was a handsome, lively, friendly young man. The farmer's wife served him dinner. Afterwards he strolled around the farm. He saw a tiny hut, with a locked door. Curiosity led him to look through the keyhole.

He gasped, amazed. There was a girl, beautiful beyond belief, and richly dressed. He fell in love immediately with her noble, sad, modest face, and hurried to the farmhouse to ask her name.

There he was told that the hut was the home of Donkey-Skin, a girl so dirty none but the pigs could stay near her.

The prince realized that these people knew nothing of the mystery. He asked no more, and went home. But he was haunted by the memory of the lovely vision he had seen, and soon he fell desperately ill of a high fever. The doctors were helpless. "Perhaps," they said to the queen, "your son has a secret sorrow."

The queen begged her son to say what troubled him. She promised him anything he wanted.

"Mother," he whispered, "have Donkey-Skin make me a cake with her own two hands. Maybe that will help."

Puzzled, the queen asked the courtiers who Donkey-Skin might be.

"That one?" said a courtier. "She's a horrid, filthy girl, who keeps pigs on one of your farms."

"No matter," said the queen. "Donkey-Skin exists. Therefore Donkey-Skin shall grant my son's wish. He wants a cake made by her. We must humor the sick. Have her make a cake. Quickly."

Orders went out to the farm posthaste.

Donkey-Skin had heard good things about the young prince. The queen's orders might give her a chance to show her true self. Happily, she hurried to her hut. She bathed and dressed in silvery robes. For her cake, she used the finest flour and the freshest eggs and butter. But, by accident (or perhaps on purpose, who knows?) a ring slid from her finger into the batter. When the cake was baked, she hid in her donkey-skin again. She gave the cake to a courtier, who hurried it back to the castle.

The prince was so pleased he sat up to eat. He almost choked on the ring. But, seeing it, he felt better. He now had a key to the mystery that haunted him. It was an emerald, set in a gold band so small that only the finest finger could wear it.

The prince wondered and pondered over this new clue. The more he wondered, the worse grew his fever.

When his parents heard that the boy's fever was worse, they came running. "Son," said the king, "tell us what you want. We'll get it for you somehow."

"Father," said the prince, "see this ring. It can solve all my problems. I want to marry the girl whose finger it fits, no matter who she is, princess or peasant."

The king took the ring. He sent a hundred drummers and trumpeters throughout the kingdom, with a hundred heralds. They summoned everyone to the Trying-on of the Ring. The girl who could wear the gold-set emerald was to marry the prince.

First came princesses. Then came duchesses, baronesses, and ladies. Not one could wear the ring. Then actresses and models tried, but their fingers were too fat. Then came maids, cooks, servants, and shepherdesses. They had no better luck.

At last the prince said, "What about Donkey-Skin? Has she tried?"

The courtiers laughed. One said, "No. She's too dirty to come to court."

"Fetch her," said the king. "We must omit no one."

Donkey-Skin had heard the heralds. She well knew that it was her ring that had caused all the commotion. Bathed and dressed and beautiful, she waited, quietly. When the heralds came for her, she slipped on her donkey-skin and opened the door. Joking, and poking fun, the courtiers led her to the prince.

"Do you live in the hut behind the barnyard?" he asked.

"Yes, Majesty," she replied.

"May I see your hand?" he said.

The king and queen were amazed, and the courtiers were dumbfounded, when they saw her hold out an exquisite little white hand. The ring slid on easily, a perfect fit.

The prince knelt before her to declare his love.

Blushing, and touched by his homage, she shook her shoulders a trifle. Her ugly disguise fell back and she was revealed—a most royal maiden, brilliantly dressed in a sun-colored dress. The king beamed. The queen clapped for joy. They begged her to marry their son.

Before she could answer, the Lilac Fairy came from on high, in a chariot of flowering lilac sprays. The fairy told the whole story of the brave princess.

The king and queen were pleased to know she was a well-born princess. But the prince rejoiced at her bravery, and fell twice as much in love.

Invitations for the wedding went out that very day. First on the list was the princess' father. He wasn't told who the bride would be. Every other king in the world came, too. There were kings in carriages, kings in rickshaws, kings riding tigers and elephants and eagles. The richest king of all was the bride's father. He appeared with his new wife, a lovely, sensible, widowed queen. Pleased and surprised to find his child alive, he gave the couple his blessing.

The prince's father gave his throne and crown to the prince as a wedding gift.

Their marriage was feasted throughout the country with a three-month holiday. But their love lasted longer still. Indeed, it would have lasted forever, had they not died at the end of a hundred happy years.

Kuzma and the Fox

A FARMER and his wife had a son named Kuzma. He was a good boy, but lazy. He just wouldn't work.

One day, his mother said, "That boy is useless. Maybe he'd be happier if he lived alone."

His father agreed. He made Kuzma a cabin in the woods. He gave him an old horse, five chickens, and a straggly rooster. There Kuzma lived, all by himself in the woods.

A fox came by one day, and smelled the chickens. When Kuzma went hunting, the fox sneaked into the cabin. She gobbled up a chicken and ran off.

When Kuzma got back, he missed the chicken and wondered who had taken it.

The next day, he went hunting again. He met the fox. Smiling sweetly, she said, "Going hunting, Kuzma?"

"Yes, I am" said Kuzma.

"Have fun," grinned the fox.

When he'd gone, she ran into the cabin. She gobbled up another chicken, and fled.

Kuzma came home and saw that he had lost another chicken. "Can Fox be the chicken thief?" he wondered.

Next day he locked his doors and windows before he went hunting. He met the fox again.

Smiling sweetly, she said, "Going hunting, Kuzma?"

"Yes, I am," said Kuzma.

"Have fun," grinned the fox.

She ran to the cabin and tried to get in, but the doors and windows were locked. "I'll slip down the chimney," she thought, and down the chimney she went.

Kuzma was hiding nearby, and had seen everything. He knew the fox couldn't leap up out of the chimney.

"Now I've got you!" he cried through the keyhole. "Your game is up, you thief."

"Please, good, kind Kuzma, don't kill me," cried the fox. "If you spare my life, I'll make your fortune. You'll never have to work again. All you have to do is pay me in advance for my help. Cook me one of your chickens, in good fresh butter."

Kuzma thought for a moment, then he said, "Well, why not?" He fried a chicken, and fed it to the fox. She gobbled it up.

Then she said, "Beyond this forest lies the kingdom of King Thunderboom and Queen Lightningzip. Their daughter is the world's best princess. She's beautiful, she's rich, and she's going to be your wife."

"What? No princess would marry me," said Kuzma.

"You'll see," said the fox. "I give you my word."

Fox ran straight to King Thunderboom's palace. She went in and bowed low. "Greetings, wise King Thunderboom. Greetings fair Queen Lightningzip," said the fox.

"Greetings, little fox," said the king. "What do you want?"

"Simply this," said the fox. "I have come to arrange a marriage. You have a fine girl, and I can get her a good husband."

"Why didn't he come himself? Is something wrong with him?" asked the king, amazed at the boldness of Fox.

"He can't leave home just now," said the fox. "He is much too busy. He rules all the wild animals and has to keep an eye on them."

"A ruler of animals is a strange kind of a son-in-law," said the king. "But let him send me forty times forty wolves. Then I'll consider him as a husband for my daughter."

Fox went to the timberland at the edge of the woods. She began to stagger and sing and hiccup as if she had eaten too much.

Presently a wolf saw her and said, "What a dinner you must have had!"

"Yes," said the fox. "I ate much too much at the king's animal banquet. Why weren't you there? You never saw so much fine food, and so many animals eating it."

"I love parties," said the wolf hopefully. "How about taking me there?"

"All right," said the fox. "But the king's cook won't cook just one supper. He cooks only for crowds. Tomorrow at noon bring forty times forty wolves here to me. We'll go to the palace together. What a feast we'll have!"

The next day a great band of wolves assembled in the forest. Fox led them to the king, lined up in rows of forty.

"Noble king," she said, "here are the wolves. Count them. Your future son-in-law sends them to you with his respects."

"Thank you," said the greedy king. "Put them in my stockyard. I see my future son-in-law has first-class fur animals. Why doesn't he send me as many bears?"

Thereupon Fox ran to Kuzma's cabin and said, "I'm hungry. In order to succeed I must look well fed. Fry me another chicken in fresh butter, please."

When Fox had gobbled Kuzma's chicken, she ran to the king's side of the woods. She sang and staggered and hiccupped as before, and before long a bear came up and said, "You look fat and well fed. Where have you been?"

"I've just left the king's animal banquet,"

said the fox, licking her chops. "What a feast! It's still going on."

"It is?" said the bear hopefully. "Can bears go too?"

"With me, they can," said Fox. "But the king's cook cooks only for crowds. Meet me tomorrow with forty times forty more bears. I'll lead the way to a real feast."

The next day the bears were waiting. Fox led them to the palace, and lined them up outside in rows of forty. Then she went in and said, "King, the bears are outside, with your son-in-law's respects."

The bears were put into the stockyard. "Bears and wolves are very good," said the king. "Now, how about some nice mink? Let him send me forty times forty mink, and I'll announce the engagement right away."

Fox ran to Kuzma's cabin. "You'll have to feed me again," she said. "I can't look skinny if I'm to make your fortune."

Kuzma fed her the last chicken, and the scraggly rooster as well. Then Fox ran to the river on the king's side of the woods.

She staggered and sang and hiccupped as before, and before long a mink came up and said, "You look as if you'd had too much to eat."

"Indeed, I have," said the fox. "I'm so full of trout I can hardly walk."

"Trout?" said the mink. "They're hard to get just now."

"Not at the king's banquet," said the fox. "The wolves and bears and everybody are gobbling trout by the ton."

"Why wasn't I invited?" asked the mink.

"It's not too late," said the fox. "Come and celebrate the engagement of the king's daughter. Meet me tomorrow, with forty times forty more mink. We'll go to the feast together."

The next day, the king was richer by forty times forty mink. When they were safely in the stockyard the king said, "Tell the young man to come tomorrow. The engagement is official. He's invited to dinner."

The next day Fox, looking busy and important, said to the king, "My master begs to be excused. He couldn't come today."

"Why not?" asked the king.

"He wants to give you half his gold. He's getting it ready, but he has nothing big enough to measure it with. He wants you to lend him a dozen bushel-baskets, so the work will go faster."

"Baskets?" gasped the king. "Yes, I'll lend him the baskets." He was tremendously impressed by anyone with gold enough to measure by the basket.

Next day Fox ran again to the palace. She said, "King, your son-in-law will arrive today. He's decided to bring all his gold. Then you may take whatever you want of it."

The delighted king arranged a big reception.

Fox ran to Kuzma's cabin. "This is it!" she cried. "You're going to marry the daughter of King Thunderboom and Queen Lightningzip. Hurry up and get ready!"

"Are you sure you're not crazy?" said Kuzma. "How can I visit a king? I don't even own a good suit."

"Forget that," said the fox. "Saddle up your old nag, and bring along a saw. Leave the rest to me."

Kuzma obeyed. He trotted behind the fox until they came to the bridge over the river near the king's palace.

"See the pillars that hold up the bridge?" Fox asked. "Go and saw them almost through."

Kuzma sawed away. Soon the beams cracked, and the bridge crashed into the river.

"Now," said Fox, "undress. Send your horse home. Let the river wash away your clothes. Stay in the water till you're blue with cold.

Then climb onto that rock out there in mid-stream. And wait for me. It's the last work you'll ever have to do, I promise."

Kuzma scratched his head, but he obeyed.

Fox ran to the palace screaming, "Sire! Good king! Help! Horror! What a tragedy! All is lost. He's drowned!"

"What's the matter?" cried the king.

"You know the bridge that leads into your kingdom? It's gone. It fell into bits under the weight of your son-in-law's gold. He fell into the water. Gold, horses, servants, himself — all are lost," panted the fox.

The king was horrified, and ashamed that his bridge had caused such trouble. He sent servants with piles of dry clothing to look for his son-in-law.

The servants found Kuzma shivering on the rock. They got him ashore, rubbed him warm and dressed him in royal garments.

When the king saw Kuzma, tall, handsome, well-dressed, and still alive, he welcomed him warmly. He apologized for having failed to make a special bridge strong enough to carry gold, horses, and many servants. Graciously, Kuzma forgave him.

Bells rang, cannon sounded a salute, everyone cheered. And Kuzma married the king's daughter.

From then on, Kuzma lived gaily with his delightful wife, in his father-in-law's delightful palace. Fox came to court to stay. Kuzma fed her chicken fried in fresh butter until the end of her days.

Puss in Boots

Once upon a time, a miller had three sons. When he died, he left the eldest son a mill, and the second a donkey. The third son got a cat.

The third son mused sadly, "My brothers have a mill and a donkey. If they work together, they can earn a living. But what am I to do, with nothing but a cat?"

The cat overheard him. He was a serious cat, and wanted to be useful. "Don't worry, master," he said. "Just get me a sack and a pair of high boots. Things are better than you think."

The third son scratched his ear doubtfully. Then he did as Puss asked.

Puss pulled on the boots, slung the sack over his shoulder, and made for a nearby briar patch.

Hundreds of rabbits lived there. Puss put some grain in his sack, then he stretched out beside it to wait.

Soon a silly young rabbit hopped into the sack to get the grain. Puss quickly drew tight the cords of the sack, and brought his booty to the king's palace. He bowed low before the king. "Sire," he said, "my lord, the Marquis of Carabas, sends you this fine rabbit."

"Thank him for me," said the king.

The next week, Puss hid with his sack in a wheat field. He caught two pheasants and presented them to the king, who thanked the marquis, and gave Puss a coin for his trouble.

For months, Puss continued to bring to the king frequent gifts of game from the Marquis of Carabas, which was the name he had decided to give his master. One day, Puss heard that the king would go driving along by the river with his daughter, the prettiest princess alive.

Puss said to his master, "Today's the day. If you do as I suggest, your fortune's made. Go for a swim in the river. And leave the rest up to me."

Into the river the young man went, without knowing why. As the king's carriage went by, Puss shouted, "Help, help, the Marquis of Carabas is drowning!"

When the king saw his old friend Puss, he sent men to aid the marquis.

Puss told the king that thieves had stolen all the marquis' clothes. (In fact, Puss had hidden them under a rock.) The king kindly sent his men to bring some of his own clothes for the marquis.

The marquis, in clothes from the king's wardrobe, was a handsome sight. The princess fell quite in love with him. The king invited him to join them for a drive.

Puss dashed ahead. He came to a field of men haying, and cried, "When the king asks, tell him this field belongs to the Marquis of Carabas. If you don't, you'll be chopped up into fine pieces."

The king came, and asked whose the field was. The men replied, as if with one voice, "It belongs to the Marquis of Carabas."

"A fine property," beamed the king.

By then, Puss had met some harvesters. "Harvesters," he shouted, "when the king asks, tell him this land belongs to the Marquis of Carabas. If you don't, you'll be chopped up into fine pieces."

Again the king asked to whom the field belonged. The men answered, as if with one voice, "This land belongs to the Marquis of Carabas."

The king congratulated the marquis once more.

All along the road, Puss ran ahead, shouting his orders. The king was impressed to see how much land the marquis owned.

The river road led to a castle. Here lived an awful ogre, the real owner of all the land along the river. Puss politely asked to be allowed to pay his respects to the famous lord of the castle.

The ogre invited him in.

Puss said, "I've heard so much about your magical powers, sire. They say you can become any animal you like, even a lion. Is it true?"

Yes," said the ogre. "Look!" He became a huge lion, just like that.

Terrified, Puss ran up to the rafters.

When the ogre stopped being a lion, Puss came down, and said, "Well done, sire! But I hear you can do something even harder. They say you can become a tiny creature, like a rat or a mouse. Frankly, I can't believe it."

"Oh, can't you?" roared the ogre. "See here." He turned into a small mouse.

Quick as a flash, Puss ate him up.

Just then, he heard the king's carriage come down the road. He sped out, flung wide the gates, and cried, "Welcome, Majesty, to the home of the Marquis of Carabas!"

"What a splendid residence, Marquis!" said the king.

"Won't you honor it, and me, by entering?" said the marquis, bowing low.

In the dining hall, a feast was spread. The ogre had invited company that day. But at the sight of the king's carriage, all the guests ran off. So the king, the princess, and the marquis dined well.

The king was charmed by the excellent qualities of the young marquis. He saw that his dear daughter was more than charmed. He said, "Marquis, I'd like you for my son-in-law."

The marquis was overjoyed. He married the princess that very day. Puss in Boots became their Prime Minister, and never had to chase rats again, except for fun.

Thumbelina

ONCE upon a time there was a woman who wanted a tiny, tiny child. She had no idea how to get one, so she went to see a witch.

"Witch," she asked, "how can I find a tiny, tiny child?"

"Easy," said the witch. "Here's a rye seed. It's not ordinary farmer's rye. It's very special. Plant it in a pot, and you'll see."

"Thank you," said the woman. She gave the witch a gold coin, went home, and planted the rye seed.

A bud on a long stem sprang up, tall as a tulip.

"What a pretty flower," said the woman. She kissed the red-gold bud and the petals popped open. There, at the golden center of the flower sat a tiny, tiny child. She was exquisite, as tall as your thumb. Thumbelina was her name.

The woman painted half a nutshell for Thumbelina's bed. It had a mattress of violets, and rosepetal covers. In the daytime Thumbelina played on the table. She went swimming in a flower bowl, or sailed in a tulip petal. All the while she sang quietly in a small, true voice.

One night as she slept, cozy in her bed, a squat frog plopped through the open window. "There's a perfect wife for my son," thought the frog.

She took Thumbelina, bed and all, in her wide mouth. Down to the brook she hopped. Mother Frog lived in the muddy bank with her son, who was fat and wet as his mother.

"Brek ekek ko-ax," was all he could say, even when he saw so pretty a girl.

"Quiet," said his mother. "You'll wake her. Come float the shell out to a lily pad. It'll be like an island. She won't escape from it till we've fixed a house for you two, here in the mud."

They put the shell out on the farthest lily pad, and swam back to their hole in the mud.

Thumbelina woke early. She saw nothing but water between her and the shore. She was frightened, and began to cry.

Presently the frogs swam out to get the nutshell bed. They wanted to put it in the mud house they were making ready for the bride. "Thumbelina, here's my son," said Mama Frog. "He'll be your husband. We're fixing you a mud house. When we've finished, you'll marry him."

"Brek ekek ko-ax," said her stupid son.

They swam away with the bed. The fish under the lily pad had heard Mama Frog's words, and they heard Thumbelina weeping and saying, "I don't want to marry him."

The fish felt sorry for the tiny child. They gathered around the underwater stem of the lily pad and they nibbled, nibbled, nibbled, till the stem was bitten through.

The lily pad began to move, like a raft. It floated down the river. Safe away it went, where the frogs couldn't follow. Sun danced gold on the water. It was a pretty day.

But alas! a dragonfly flew by and seized Thumbelina around her tiny, tiny waist. He carried her up to a tree. There he put her on a big leaf, and told her she was pretty. When the other beetles came, they said she wasn't pretty at all, for she had only two legs, and no wings. She was too much like people, who are the insects' worst enemies, said the jealous lady dragonflies. So the dragonfly carried her down to the ground and left her there.

All summer, Thumbelina lived alone in the forest. She wove a grassblade hammock, and slung it under a Queen Anne's lace flower that kept off the rain. She gathered pollen to eat. Every morning she drank dew from the leaves.

Summer and fall were a happy adventure for Thumbelina. But winter came. The birds went south. The trees and flowers lost their leaves. The Queen Anne's lace drooped, dried, and died.

Thumbelina was cold clear through. Her clothes were ragged. She was so tiny and fragile she almost died of cold. It began to snow, and each flake that fell on her was like a big ball of snow would be to someone your size. Shivering, Thumbelina wrapped herself up in a dry leaf.

Near the forest lay a wide field, where wheat stubble stood up from the frozen ground. Thumbelina went there, looking for shelter. To her, the cut stalks were tall as trees. She saw a little door. It was the house of a field mouse. She knocked at the door, and begged the field mouse for a grain of wheat to eat.

"Poor child," said the mouse, who was a kind old creature. "Come where it's warm, and eat with me."

She saw how sweet Thumbelina was, and said, "Why don't you stay all winter? You can clean house, and tell me stories."

So Thumbelina stayed, and they lived content together. "I'm expecting a visitor, one of these days," said the mouse. "My neighbor, Mole, comes every week. He's rich and wise. He has a big house, and wears a black velvet coat. If you could marry him, you'd never want for anything. He lives alone, and he's almost blind. He'd like to hear you tell your stories. Don't

mind if he says mean things about the birds and flowers, for he's never seen them. He hates the sun."

Mole did come calling, in his black velvet coat. Mouse said, "Please sing for us, Thumbelina."

So Thumbelina sang, and Mole fell in love with her lovely voice. But he was too dignified to come right out and say so.

Mole had just dug a new tunnel to Mouse's house. He said, "Mouse, you and your guest may use it freely. Someone buried a dead bird in it yesterday. But don't be afraid. He's quite whole, and frozen with cold."

Mole made a hole in the tunnel roof over the bird's head, so they would be able to see it, and step over it. Thumbelina was sad to see the pretty bird lying so cold and quiet.

But Mole kicked the bird, and said, "There's one who won't screech any more. All a bird is good for is to sing, sing, sing, until winter comes. Then he has to change his tune. He doesn't prepare for the cold."

"Yes," said Mouse. "You're wonderfully prudent. Birds aren't. They think only of singing."

Thumbelina thought, "They only sing, it's true. But their singing is one of the world's joys."

That night Thumbelina could not sleep for thinking of the poor frozen bird. She took a woven grass cover and an armful of cotton wisps out to the tunnel. She tucked them carefully around the bird. She couldn't bear to think of him lying cold in the lonely dark.

"Farewell, dear bird," she said. "Thank you for your summer songs." She stroked his soft breast, saying good-by.

Then she jumped! She heard a beating, faint and quick. She listened again. It was the bird's heart! He wasn't dead. Most swallows fly to the warm south when winter comes. But this one had stayed and been stunned by the cold. The warm covers had made him stir again.

Thumbelina was frightened, for the bird was much bigger than she. Bravely she ran to get the cover from her own bed, and she tucked it carefully around the swallow.

Next night she went to the tunnel again. The bird was very weak, but he was alive. "Thank you, tiny, tiny child," he said. "Soon I'll be strong. I'll fly off into the sunlight again."

"Oh, but you can't," cried Thumbelina. "It's snowing outside, and bitter cold. Stay warm here, until spring. I'll take care of you."

She brought him water in a leaf, and grain to eat. Mole and Mouse never guessed it, but all winter Thumbelina cared for the swallow.

When spring came Swallow said, "Soon I'll fly off. Will you come with me, Thumbelina? I can carry you easily on my back."

"I mustn't make dear Mouse sad," said Thumbelina. "She's been so kind. I can't go."

"Then farewell, tiny, tiny girl, and thank you," said the swallow. With a sharp cry of joy, Swallow darted into the upper air, and was gone.

One day Mouse said, "Today we'll start making your wedding clothes. You'll marry Mole in the fall, lucky girl."

Four spiders spun thread for fine cloth. Thumbelina and Mouse worked all summer long, making a lovely trousseau. Every time Thumbelina could go out of doors, she looked for her swallow friend. But she never saw him.

Summer came to an end. Thumbelina would marry Mole in a few days. One day she stood outside the mouse house and held out her arms. "Good-by, bright earth," she said. "Good-by, skies. Good-by, sun and trees and flowers and fresh breezes."

Just then she heard, "Queet, queet," high

above her in the air. She looked up. There was the swallow, flying to her. When he heard that Thumbelina didn't want to marry Mole, he said, "Come with me, instead."

"Yes," said Thumbelina, "I'll come." She climbed on his back, and tied herself to his strong feathers with her sash. Up went Swallow, up, up, into the bright air. Over mountains they flew, over seas.

Far to the south the air was warm. The sky seemed higher, and full of a lovely light. Below, Thumbelina saw oranges and lemons growing on trees.

Swallow flew on and on. Soon, the sea below was a blaze of clear blue. Along its shore grew tall trees. In the shade of the trees were the ruins of a white marble castle. Vines flowered around its broken columns. In its eaves were dozens of swallow nests.

Thumbelina's friend lived in one of those nests. "There's my home," said Swallow. "And see, there are beautiful flowers just below. Shall I put you down? It would suit you. You'll surely find a good house there."

"It's perfect," said Thumbelina, clapping her hands.

Swallow put Thumbelina gently down on the wide petals of a beautiful white flower. Thumbelina looked around her, enchanted.

And then she stared. For at the flower's heart sat a tiny, tiny prince. He wore a gold crown, and on his shoulders were shining white wings. He was no bigger than Thumbelina. He was the spirit of the flower.

Each flower had its own spirit, and he was ruler of them all.

"Isn't he handsome?" whispered Thumbelina to Swallow.

The prince wasn't too sure he liked the huge bird. But when he saw Thumbelina he was enchanted. She was the loveliest girl he had ever seen. He took off his gold crown and put it on Thumbelina's head.

"What's your name?" he asked. "And please, will you be my wife? You'd be a perfect queen for my flower kingdom, and I do love you so."

"Yes," said Thumbelina. "I'll marry you. My name is Thumbelina."

The spirits of the other flowers came flying to her, bearing gifts. The best present was a pair of lovely transparent wings. With them Thumbelina could fly among the flowers as much as she wished.

"Thumbelina's not a pretty enough name for a girl as lovely as you," said the prince. "We'll call you Maia."

Swallow watched from his nest above. He sang and sang his very best, for he was glad the tiny, tiny girl had found a good home at last.

One day Swallow sang, "Queet, queet, good-by, good-by." Away he flew to the north, where he spent his summers. His summer nest was above the window of a storyteller. There he sang, "Queet, queet." And that's how we happen to know the tale of the tiny, tiny girl who was called Thumbelina.

Green Snake

Once upon a time, a queen had twin baby girls. She invited a dozen fairies to visit. In those days, when fairies came to call, they made gifts to the new babies. They often turned ordinary infants into marvels of wit and grace. But sometimes parents who sought fairy gifts got more than they bargained for.

A magnificent banquet was prepared for the fairies. As they were about to sit down, Old Mag appeared. She was the meanest of a family of mean fairies.

The queen shook in her slippers. Old Mag, who hadn't been invited, was sure to be insulted. Who knew what she might do?

The queen quickly brought Old Mag a jeweled chair. The fairy said, rudely, "I don't need that. I'm tall enough, standing up." But her eyes scarcely reached as high up as the table top. The position was most uncomfortable, and made her crosser than ever.

"Please, do take a chair and sit down," begged the queen.

"If you'd wanted me to sit at your table, you'd have invited me," said Mag. "Well, I may be old and ugly. But my magic is as powerful as if I were pretty. Maybe more so."

At last she consented to sit down. Then she saw each of the other fairies had a corsage of jewels. There was no corsage for her. Instead, the queen brought her a ruby box crammed with diamonds.

Old Mag snapped, "Keep your junk. I already own more jewels than I want. You've proved that you never meant to invite me."

She banged her wand on the table. The delicious food turned into plates full of sizzled snakes. The other fairies jumped up and ran, horrified.

As they went, Old Mag hurried to the first baby's crib. "I give you," she spat, "the gift of being absolutely hideous."

As she started for the second crib, the other fairies ran in and held her back. That made her furious. She flew *smash!* through the window on a bolt of lightning.

The other fairies gave the first baby the best gifts they could. But the queen wept, as her baby grew uglier by the minute.

"How can we comfort her?" the fairies wondered. They whispered together. "Majesty," they said, "don't cry. We promise that one day your baby will be the happiest girl alive."

"But will she be beautiful?" sobbed the queen.

"We may not explain," they said, "but trust us. She'll be happy."

The queen thanked them, and gave them armloads of presents. Although fairies have everything, they like presents very much.

The queen named the first twin Dorugly, and the second, Dorabelle. The names were apt. Dorugly grew up ugly indeed. Dorabelle was a very pretty girl.

When Dorugly was twelve years old, she wanted to leave court. The king owned a deserted castle where she could live unseen, and her parents agreed to let her go there.

She left with her dear old nurse, and a few servants. The ancient castle was at the sea's edge. There were woods on both sides, and wide fields behind. There she lived alone for two years. She practiced her music and drawing. She even wrote two books of poems.

But she felt lonely for her parents, and one day she drove back to their court. She arrived just in time to see the merry wedding of her sister, Dorabelle, to a neighboring king.

Her family was far from glad to see her. Hardly anyone spoke to her, except to say, "Dorugly, you're much uglier these days. That face of yours should be hidden. It's enough to spoil the wedding guests' enjoyment."

Poor Dorugly said quietly, "I hadn't meant to interfere. I just missed you all. But you don't want to see me. I'll leave right away."

Dorugly felt like losing her temper, and

telling them that her ugliness was not her fault, but theirs. But she was wise, and hid her hurt. With her faithful nurse, she went back to her castle.

One day as she was walking in the forest, she came on a great green snake. It reared its crested head, and said, "Good morning, Dorugly. Don't be sad. Look at me. I'm uglier than you. Yet I was once very handsome."

Dorugly was too frightened to hear. She ran home, and stayed inside for days. But one evening, tired of her rooms, she went walking by the sea. Out of nowhere, with no one aboard, sailed a fantastic little boat. It was golden, and painted in delightful designs. Its masts and oars were of cedar, and its sails were of gold brocade.

It drifted in to the water's edge, and Dorugly climbed aboard to see it better. She went into the tiny cabin, which was hung with scarlet velvet draped on diamond nails. She was charmed, until she noticed the boat was drifting out to sea.

Dorugly seized the oars, and tried to row. But the wind took her out of sight of the land. She thought, "I'll surely die, and I should be glad. I'm so ugly, everyone hates me. My sister's a queen. But I'm just a hermit. Only horrid snakes talk to me."

Just then, in fact, a green snake swam over the waves. It called, "If you'd let a horrid snake help, I could save your life."

"I'd sooner die," said Dorugly, who was afraid of snakes.

Without a word, Green Snake vanished under the waves.

"That horrid green creature scares me," thought Dorugly. "I shake when I see those ivory claws, and bronze wings, and fiery eyes. I'd rather die than owe him my life. But why does he follow me? How did he learn to talk?"

Out of the air, a voice replied, "Princess, be kinder to Green Snake. After all, he's handsome, for a snake; while you are ugly, for a girl. He can help you more than you suppose, if you will only let him."

A big gust of wind came just then and drove the boat against a rock, and it broke into a thousand pieces. Dorugly managed to snatch a piece as it floated by. Holding it tight, she stayed afloat until she could get a foothold on the rock.

She almost fainted when she saw that she had held, not a piece of wood, but Green Snake.

He swam off a little way when he saw she was afraid. "You'd fear me less if you knew me better," he called, and then he vanished.

Dorugly was alone on the enormous rock. "I'm safe from the sea," she thought. "But on this rock, I'll probably starve to death." Night was coming. She climbed as high as she could. Then she made a pillow of her apron, and went woefully to sleep.

As she slept, the sound of soft music came to her ears. Dorugly thought that she was dreaming. But imagine her astonishment when she opened her eyes!

The rock, and the sea, were gone. She was on a golden couch in a golden room. Outside was a golden balcony. Wondering, she went out on the balcony to look around. Before her spread gardens, parks, and woods. There were graceful fountains and statues, and hundreds of jeweled houses. On the calm sea below boats sailed busily.

"Where am I?" exclaimed Dorugly. "Is it possible that a snake saved me from drowning, only yesterday?"

There was a knock, and she went to the door. She looked down at a delightful, strange sight. Fifty tiny Chinese dolls, come to life,

smiled up at her. They were less than a foot tall and of every possible shape. Some were pretty, some comical, some unusual. Some were made of diamonds, some of crystal and diamonds, some of pearls, some of crystal and ruby, some of ruby, some of porcelain.

The dolls had come to welcome Dorugly to their charming kingdom. Their leader was a ruby doll.

"My lady," he said, "our king wishes us to make your stay as happy as we can. We are his messengers. We go about the world, pretending to be lifeless figurines. We bring back the latest inventions and news, to amuse our king. We're at your orders, my lady, if only you'll stay with us."

They showed her the way to the gardens, where she found a fine swimming pool. Under a royal green pavilion stood two gold chairs.

"Whose are those?" asked Dorugly.

"One is for our king. The other is yours, my lady," said the ruby doll.

"But where is the king?" asked Dorugly.

"He is away at the wars," answered the doll.

"Is he married?" asked Dorugly.

"No," said the doll. "He's never met a girl to share his high ideals."

Dorugly went for a swim in the beautiful pool. Then the pearl doll helped her into a silk dressing-gown. A set of dolls paraded ahead of her, playing instruments made from nutshells. They led her to her room. More dolls combed and dressed her hair, and brought her splendid clothes. The dolls were the wisest, wittiest, most kindly friends imaginable. For the first time in her life, Dorugly enjoyed being a princess.

A week in such company made Dorugly's sweet, bright disposition come to life, and all the dolls grew to love her dearly.

One night, as she lay in her bed, she wondered, "What next? This is a wonderful life. But my heart feels empty, for some reason."

"You'd know the reason, my lady, if you'd learn to love," said a voice from the air. "True joy comes only to those who love."

"Which doll is speaking?" asked the princess.

"No doll. I am the king of this land, my lady. And I love you dearly."

"A king loves me?" Dorugly said. "You'd have to be blind. I'm the ugliest thing alive."

"I have seen you, and I disagree. Anyway, I adore you," said the voice.

"You're very kind," said Dorugly. "I hardly know what to say. The idea is too new."

The invisible king said no more that night. Next day, Dorugly didn't want to discuss him with the dolls. But she did ask if the king had come home.

They said, "No." This puzzled her.

"Is he a young man, and handsome?" she asked.

"Yes," they answered, "and charming, too. We get news of him every day."

"But does he know I'm here?" Dorugly wondered.

"Yes, my lady," said the ruby doll. "He knows all about you. A messenger goes every hour of the day to bring him word of how you are."

From then on, Dorugly often heard the king's voice when she was alone. He said such kind things she forgot to be afraid.

One dark night she awoke to see a dim figure near her bed. Thinking it her friend the pearl doll, she put out her hand. But the hand was held, and kissed, and tears fell on it. She knew it must be the king.

"What do you expect of me?" she said. "How can I learn to love you, if I've never seen you?"

"My princess, I can't show myself to you. Wicked Old Mag, who was so cruel to you,

laid a seven-year curse on me. Five years have passed. Two years of her curse are left. They'd be happy years, if you'd agree to marry me now."

No one could deny the kindness and generosity of the invisible king. Dorugly began to feel love and gratitude fill her heart. She agreed to marry the king. She promised she wouldn't try to see him until the two years were up. "You see, my dear," he said, "should you try to see me, the seven years of my curse would begin all over. And you'd have to share in my punishment. You'll get bad advice, and be tempted to break your promise. If you keep your promise, a glad day will come. I'll be as handsome as you'd want, and you'll get back the beauty Old Mag took from you."

Dorugly had never dared hope for such joy. She vowed to be an obedient wife, absolutely without curiosity. Soon they were quietly married.

Months later, Dorugly got the notion that she must invite her family to visit them. The king tried to change her mind. But she wouldn't listen. Finally, they sent a party of dolls, bearing gifts and an invitation, to Dorugly's mother who was far over the seas.

Her mother was very curious to see Dorugly and her husband. She came at once, with Dorabelle.

Dorugly enjoyed showing them her palace and her pretty kingdom. When they asked for her husband, she made up excuses. But she was too honest to lie cleverly. One day, she said her husband was off on a pilgrimage. Another day, she said he was ill, or fighting a war, or out hunting. Her mother and sister suspected she had no husband at all. They began to tease her.

Finally, Dorugly told them the truth.

They talked and talked and talked, until Dorugly began to worry. She said, "I've never

seen him. Yet every word he says proves how good and charming he is. And in two years, I'll see him. I'll even be freed of Old Mag's curse, and be beautiful again."

"Poor simple fool!" cried her mother. "Do you believe a promise like that? He tricked you into marriage. He's probably a monster of some kind."

While her mother was there, Dorugly defended her husband. But when she'd sent her mother home, loaded with rich presents, she worried. She was confused and curious. One night, she took a lamp and lit it to steal a glance at her dear husband.

One look, and she shrieked in dismay. It was no young prince she saw, but Green Snake.

He was heartbroken at her cry. "Why do you treat me so badly, though I've loved you well?" he asked sadly.

Dorugly heard nothing, for she had fainted with fright.

Green Snake disappeared.

The dolls came running. They tried to calm Dorugly. But then a doll watchman arrived with bad news. Old Mag had just led a fleet of warships, manned by marionettes, into the port.

The dolls fought bravely against the marionettes. Punch led Old Mag's army, and Judy led her fleet. To amuse herself Old Mag let the battle rage for a while.

Then she waved her wand. The dolls vanished. Their pretty city, their parks, palaces, houses, and all fell into dust.

Only Dorugly remained and she was at Old Mag's mercy.

And of mercy Old Mag had none, as Dorugly was soon to discover. The marionette army brought the captive queen to the old fairy. "Queen, we've met before," Old Mag snarled. "I was insulted, once, on your account."

"Haven't you punished me enough? It wasn't my fault," said Dorugly. "And your curse of ugliness has already done me great harm."

"You talk too much," said Old Mag. "Punch, get me that pair of iron shoes. Put them on the queen."

Punch brought a pair of iron shoes as narrow as your finger. He had no pity, but jammed Dorugly's feet into them.

Then Old Mag handed Dorugly a horrid spindle, wound with a tangled mass of spider webs. "Spin it strong and fine and straight. And hurry. I want it done in two hours."

"I don't know how to spin," said Dorugly. "But I'll try."

They pushed her into a dark cave, and shut its opening with a rock.

Dorugly tried to spin. A hundred times the dirty webs broke under her touch. Patiently she tried, over and over. But it was no use. She thought of the happy life her curiosity had spoiled, and wept.

Suddenly came a voice from out of nowhere. "My queen, you brought misery on yourself and me. But I love you. I won't let you suffer. I've one friend left. Her name is Fairy Protectress. Look to her for help."

A sharp rap sounded three times. Dorugly saw no one. But she looked, and there was her thread spun and wound, neat as could be.

After two hours, Old Mag came in, ready for trouble. "Let's see your work, you lazy, stupid girl," she croaked.

"I've done my best," said Dorugly, handing her the ball of thread.

"You think you're clever, don't you?" shrieked Old Mag, furious and amazed. "We'll see. Make your spider-thread into nets strong enough to catch salmon. If you fail, you're lost."

"But my lady," said Dorugly, "even flies can sometimes break spiderwebs."

Old Mag went out, unheeding. The marionettes once more closed over the cave with a rock.

"Fairy Protectress, if you feel any pity for me, help me now," cried Dorugly.

Before she'd finished speaking, the thread wove itself into a sturdy net. Gratitude filled Dorugly. She thanked Fairy Protectress and added, "Green Snake, my king, how generous you are to love me still! I'm sorry I disobeyed you. I'm sorry I've hurt you."

When Old Mag saw the perfect net, she was angry. "I'll take you to my kingdom. There, no one will help you," she cried. Her marionettes chained Dorugly and put her aboard Old Mag's boat. Old Mag laughed to see the queen weep, and told Punch to set sail.

That night, Dorugly looked up at the stars, and longed to be free. Green Snake's voice called to her. He swam close to the ship, and said, "Don't worry. I love you, and we'll find a way."

"How can you forgive my wicked curiosity?" whispered Dorugly.

But Old Mag overheard them. She never slept, when she had a chance to do harm.

"Green Snake," she cried, "I command you to stay out the time of your curse in a dark hole at the world's end. As for you, Dorugly, wait till we come to my kingdom. You'll see."

Green Snake swam off, sighing, toward his prison. The next day, the ship docked. Old Mag pushed Dorugly ashore. She chained a millstone to her neck, and gave her a pitcher full of holes.

"Now, Queen, climb that mountain over there. There's a valley beyond it, full of wild animals. They guard the Well of Discretion. Go to the well, and bring me back that pitcher full of its water." Old Mag cackled. "And mind you hurry," she added. "I give you three years."

Dorugly said, "I can't move this millstone. The pitcher's full of holes. It won't hold water. How can I obey?"

"I don't care how. Obey, or else I'll make Green Snake suffer," Old Mag said.

The threat to poor, brave Green Snake was more than Dorugly could bear. She forgot everything else. She tried to start her impossible job.

Fairy Protectress rewarded her unselfishness. The air itself lifted Dorugly over the mountain, and set her down in the Valley of Beasts. The good fairy tamed the wild beasts with a wave of her wand. At another wave of the wand appeared a chariot, drawn by two birds.

Dorugly tried to thank the fairy, who smiled, and said, "Green Snake asked me to help you. The birds will carry you to the Well of Discretion. They'll fill your pitcher for you, too. When you have the Water of Discretion, wash your face. You will be beautiful again."

"How wonderful!" said Dorugly.

"But you mustn't return to Old Mag right away. Your curse puts you under her power for seven years. The birds will bring you to a forest. Live out your curse there, in peace."

Queen Dorugly said, "I thank you with all my heart. But all your gifts, even beauty, can't make me truly glad. I can't be happy while Green Snake suffers."

"If you are brave for the seven years of your curse, you'll be free, and Green Snake, too, my dear."

"Shall I have no news of him in the forest?" asked Dorugly.

"For the harm your curiosity did you deserve to spend the rest of your life without news of him," said the fairy softly.

Dorugly knew it was true. Tears of remorse came to her eyes. She got into her chariot and the birds took her to the Well of Discretion.

Very cleverly they patched up her pitcher, and filled it with the water.

Dorugly thought, "Perhaps this water can make me wise. I'd rather drink and grow sensible, than wash to be beautiful. If I'd been sensible, I'd still be living as a queen with my king."

She drank some of the water first. Then she washed her face. She grew so lovely the very air was radiant around her.

The good fairy appeared, and said, "Your wish to be more wise than beautiful pleases me. Because of it, I will shorten your punishment to three years."

"I don't deserve it," said Dorugly. "If you can lift curses, help Green Snake instead."

"I'll try," said Fairy Protectress. "How beautiful you are! You can no longer be called Dorugly. I name you Queen Discreet."

Before she left, the fairy replaced the queen's cruel iron shoes with a pair of embroidered slippers.

The birds brought Queen Discreet to the forest. There, trees roofed over the leaf-carpeted ground. Waterfalls and brooks sang sweetly. Best of all, there were animals that could talk.

They welcomed the birds. "We thought you'd forgotten us," said a mole.

"Fairy Protectress has sent us a guest," said the birds. "This is Queen Discreet."

"How beautiful you are!" they cried. "Will you please be our queen?"

"Yes, if you wish," said the queen graciously. "Tell me, what sort of place is this?"

The mole answered, "Not long ago, some fairies got tired of all the naughtiness in the world. First, they asked people to be good. That didn't work, so they used magic spells instead. Piggish men became pigs. Gossipy girls became parrots or hens. Those who teased became monkeys. This wood is their home,

until the fairies decide they've learned their lesson."

The forest folk loved Queen Discreet. They fed her fruits and nuts, and amused her with their stories. The queen might have been perfectly happy in this pleasant place. But she never stopped regretting the disobedient curiosity that had done such harm to Green Snake.

Three years passed quickly. Queen Discreet once again put on her iron shoes. She took her pitcher full of the Water of Discretion, and her millstone, and the birds brought her to Old Mag.

Old Mag gave an amazed screech to see her. She had hoped the queen dead or lost forever. But there she stood, alive as ever.

"Here is your water," said Queen Discreet.

As Old Mag took the pitcher, she saw the queen's face. She screeched again, this time in rage. "What made you beautiful?" she cried.

"I washed in the Water of Discretion," replied the queen.

"You dare defy me?" said Old Mag, stamping her foot. "I'll teach you. Walk in your iron shoes to the world's end. There, in a dark prison hole, is a bottle of the Essence of Long Life. Bring it to me. I forbid you to open the bottle. If you disobey, your curse will last forever."

Tears came to Queen Discreet's eyes. Old Mag saw them and laughed nastily. "Run along," she sneered. "I know you just love to obey me."

The queen walked a long way, not knowing where to turn to find the world's end. Tired at last, she lay down, and dreamed of Green Snake.

Fairy Protectress appeared, and said, "Queen Discreet, do you know that you can free Green Snake from Old Mag, if you bring her the Essence of Long Life?"

"I'd go if I could," said the queen. "But the

Essence of Long Life is in a dark hole at the world's end. I don't know how to get there."

"Take this leafy branch," said the fairy. "Strike the ground with it."

Thankfully, the queen obeyed. The earth opened before her. Down a dim path she went, into the dark hole where Green Snake was imprisoned. She was still afraid of snakes. But she went bravely ahead.

Her courage was rewarded. She came upon the handsomest young man she'd ever seen. She knew then that it must be Green Snake.

He was so dazzled by her new beauty, and so glad to see her, that he was speechless.

Their hearts brimmed with joy. They asked the witch who had guarded Green Snake for the Essence of Long Life. She gave the queen a bottle. Its cork was loose, just to tempt her curiosity. But Queen Discreet had learned her lesson. Never again would curiosity make her do wrong.

The king and queen hurried back to Old Mag. Old Mag took the bottle of the Essence of Long Life, and drained it dry in one gulp. It did her so much good that she forgave all her enemies.

With a wave of her wand, Old Mag built up Green Snake's ruined kingdom, dolls and all. Then she sent Green Snake and his beautiful queen home.

There they lived merrily, twenty times longer than their miseries had lasted.

The Tinder Box

A SOLDIER came down the road one night. He walked as if he were marching, one, two, one, two. His duffle bag was on his back. His sword was at his side. He'd been to the wars. Now he was going home.

On the road, he met a witch. She was an awful sight. Just imagine, she had lips that dangled down to her waist.

"Hello, soldier," she said. "What a big bag you have! What a big sword you have! You're a real soldier, I must say."

"Thank you, witch," said the soldier.

"Do you see that big tree by the road?" she asked. "It's hollow inside. There's a hole at the top. If you climb up, you can drop down inside, right to the bottom of the tree. I'll put a rope around your waist, and pull you out when you're ready."

"What would I do at the bottom of the tree?" asked the soldier.

"You'd get money," said the witch. "At the bottom of the tree you will find yourself in a wide tunnel. It is lit by lamps. You'll see three doors with keys in their locks. In the first room is a big chest and on top of it sits a dog. His eyes are big as saucers. That mustn't stop you. Take my apron along. Spread it on the floor. Pick up the dog and set him on the apron. Take all the money you want from the chest. It's full of copper.

"If you want silver, go to the next room. There you'll see another dog. His eyes are as big as bicycle wheels. That mustn't stop you. Spread my apron, set the dog on it, and take the silver from the chest.

"If it's gold you want, go to the third room. The dog there has eyes big as Ferris wheels. He's quite a dog, I must say. But that mustn't stop you. Set him on my apron, and take all the gold you want from the chest."

"Not bad," said the soldier. "But what do you want out of it for yourself?"

"Not a penny," said the witch. "I only want an old tinder box my granny left down there."

"All right," said the soldier. "Tie the rope round my waist, and I'll go."

"There you are," said the witch. "And here's my apron."

The soldier climbed up the tree, and let himself down the hole. He saw the room the witch had told him of. He opened the first door.

There was a dog, staring at him with eyes big as saucers.

"Goo--oo-ood boy," said the soldier. He spread the apron, set the dog upon it, and filled his pockets with copper from the chest. Then he put back the dog, took the apron, and went to the next room.

There was a dog, staring at him with eyes big as bicycle wheels.

"If you stare too long, you'll hurt your eyes," the soldier said to the dog. He spread the apron, set the dog upon it, and opened the chest. When he saw the silver piled high in the chest, he dumped the copper he'd taken before. He filled his pockets with silver instead. Then he put back the dog, took the apron, and went to the next room.

There was a dog, staring at him with eyes big as Ferris wheels. The huge eyes were spinning dizzily in the dog's head.

"Good evening, dog," said the soldier, saluting. He'd never seen a dog like that. But he went ahead. He spread the apron, set the dog upon it, and opened the chest. When he saw all that gold, he dumped the silver he'd taken before. He filled his duffle bag, his pockets, his hat, even his socks, with gold. He had enough gold to buy all the lollipops and balloons and parks and houses in the city. He could hardly walk, with the weight of it.

He called up the tree trunk, "Pull me up, witch. I'm ready."

"Have you the tinder box?" she screeched.

"Just a minute," he called. "I almost forgot."

He got the tinder box and the witch hauled him out.

"What will you do with the tinder box, witch?" asked the soldier politely.

"None of your ding-dang business, soldier," answered the witch.

"That's no way to talk," said the soldier. "Tell me what you want it for, or I'll cut off your head."

"No," said the witch.

So he drew his sword, and cut off her head.

He took her apron to carry his money in, and shoved the tinder box back into his pocket.

Then he went to the big, beautiful city. He went to the best inn, and took the best room they had. He ordered a dinner of everything he liked best. He was a rich man now, because he had so much money.

He bought a lot of expensive clothes, and he became the most elegant man in town. He made a lot of fine friends, who told him all about the sights of the city, and especially about the king's daughter. They said she was really worth seeing.

"How can I see her?" asked the elegant soldier.

"You can't," they said. "She's locked behind walls and gardens and more walls in a big steel castle. Only the king and queen ever see her.

A fairy once said she'd marry a plain common soldier. Naturally, the king can't let that happen."

"Too bad," thought the soldier. "I'd have liked to see her." He continued to lead a gay life. He went to the theater, and to parties. He gave a lot of money to poor people, because he knew how hard it is not to have enough to eat. There were many who helped him spend his gold, and who told him he was wonderful. He liked that.

But he wasn't working at anything, except spending money. Soon he had no money left.

He moved from his excellent inn into a tiny furnished room. He mended his own shoes and clothes. He lost all his fawning friends, who only enjoyed people with money to spend.

One dark evening, he had no light. He sat in the dark, until he remembered a candle stub in his duffle bag. He got it out, along with the tinder box he'd found down the tree. He struck the tinder box.

The door opened at once, and there was the dog with eyes big as saucers. The dog said, "What does my master desire?"

"Well!" exclaimed the soldier. "What a wonderful tinder box! Dog, I'd like some money, please."

Bing! the dog was gone. And bang! he was back again, with a sackful of copper money.

The soldier knew then that the tinder box was magic. If he struck it once, the copper-chest dog came. Twice, and the silver-chest dog appeared. If he struck it three times, the gold-chest dog appeared.

He got back his excellent apartment at the inn, and his fine clothes. The friends who'd forgotten him when he was poor remembered him again.

One evening he thought, "Why can't I get to see the princess? I'd like to. They say she's

beautiful. But beauty's no use if no one sees it." Thereupon he took his tinder box and struck it once. The copper-chest dog appeared.

"It's midnight, I know," said the soldier. "But I'd like to see the princess right away."

Bing! the dog was gone. And bang! he was back. He carried the princess, fast asleep, on his back. She was so beautiful anyone could see she was a real princess. The soldier kissed her, for he was a real soldier. Then the dog brought the princess back to her castle.

At breakfast next morning the princess said to her parents, "I had a dream last night about a soldier and his dog. The dog carried me on his back, and the soldier gave me a kiss."

"What a dreadful dream," said the queen. She ordered a lady-in-waiting to guard the princess that night, for she wanted to know if it was only a dream.

The soldier wanted to see the princess again and he ordered the dog to fetch her. The dog ran fast with the princess on his back. But the lady-in-waiting saw him. She pulled on magic boots and sped after him. She saw him vanish through the soldier's window.

Quickly the lady marked a big white cross on the soldier's door. Then she went home to bed. When the dog came out with the princess, he saw the white cross. He took some chalk and marked white crosses on every door in town. No one could tell which door had been marked by the lady-in-waiting.

Early the next morning, the king and the queen and the lady went to see where the princess had been.

"There!" cried the lady-in-waiting when she saw the first door with a white cross.

"No, there!" cried the queen, when she saw the next door.

"There's another, and another," cried the king. "All the doors have white crosses."

They saw it was hopeless to try and find the soldier, and they went home.

The queen was a clever mother, and wanted to know where her daughter had been. So she filled a tiny cloth bag with flour, and sewed it in the princess' gown. Then she made a tiny hole in the bag.

The dog came again that night. He took the princess on his back and ran to the soldier, who by now loved her dearly. The dog never noticed the bag and the trail of flour leading from the palace to the soldier's window.

Next morning the king saw where his daughter had been and he quickly put the soldier in jail.

"Tomorrow you'll hang," the guards told the soldier. The soldier wasn't pleased to hear it. He had left his tinder box at home. The next morning he saw the people hurrying to the place where he was to be hung. He heard the drums begin, and the soldiers coming for him, one, two, one, two.

A cobbler passed near the cell window. "Hey there!" cried the soldier. "Don't be in such a hurry. They can't do anything until I get there. But if you'll go to my home, and bring me my tinder box, I'll give you a gold coin."

The cobbler liked the idea of good pay for short work. He scooted off and brought the tinder box to the soldier. In the public square was a big scaffold, ready to hang the soldier high. The king and queen were there to watch, along with all the court and ministers of state.

The soldier was on the scaffold with the rope round his neck when he spoke. "Condemned men are always allowed a last request," he said. "I'd like to smoke a last pipe, if I may, before you hang me."

"All right," said the king.

The soldier struck his tinder box one, and one, two, and one, two, three times. Bing! and bing! and bing! three big dogs appeared.

"Help me quickly," said the soldier, "for I'm about to be hung."

The dogs leaped on the judges. They tossed them high in the air, and let them fall squashed to the ground

"Don't!" cried the king. But the dogs took the king, and the queen as well. They tossed them high in the air, and let them fall squashed to the ground.

The soldiers were terrified. Everyone cried out, "Soldier, be our king. Make the princess your queen."

They put the soldier in the king's carriage. The dogs danced before it, and the soldiers presented arms. The princess came out of her steel castle and became queen, which pleased her very much.

The wedding feast lasted a whole week. The dogs sat at the royal table, and rolled eyes big as saucers, eyes big as bicycle wheels, and eyes big as Ferris wheels. Everyone had a very good time.

Cinderella

Once upon a time, a widower had a daughter who was wonderfully kind and good. He married a second wife who was proud, and very selfish. She had two daughters, and they were as mean as their mother.

The wedding over, the second wife no longer pretended to be pleasant. She knew well that the sweetness of her husband's child made her own daughters seem even more unpleasant. So she hated the girl, and made her work at all the meanest household tasks.

The poor girl cooked, and scrubbed, and cleaned her sloppy stepsisters' big, fancy rooms. Her own room was in a tiny, cold attic. But she never complained. She knew it would have disturbed her father, who had troubles enough.

His new wife bossed the poor man terribly.

In the evenings, she'd sit by the fire in the cinders. Her stepmother called her Cindercrawler. Her younger stepsister, not quite so mean, changed the name to Cinderella. Despite her name, she was far lovelier in rags than her stepsisters in their expensive gowns.

One day, the king's son sent invitations to a ball. The girls chattered and scurried, trying on dozens of dresses.

"I'll wear my red velvet," said the elder, "the one with real lace."

"I'll wear my plain ball gown," the other sister said. "But I have my diamonds, too. And my cape with gold flowers."

They had the best beautician in town come to the house to tell them how to do their hair. Cinderella had excellent taste, and they sent for her to ask her opinion.

"I'll do your hair, if you like," she said.

As Cinderella brushed away at their hair, they teased her. "Wouldn't you like to go to the ball, Cinderella?"

"I'm afraid a ballroom is no place for me," she answered.

"You're so right. Imagine, a Cindercrawler at a ball. How people would laugh!"

A girl less good than Cinderella would have

51

made their hair look like haystacks. But she did her best to make her stepsisters stylish. They were pleased. They were so busy primping and prancing at their mirrors that they forgot to eat. They broke dozens of laces, trying to make their waists small. But at last they were ready to leave for the ball. Cinderella watched, and when they had gone, she wept a little for loneliness. Her fairy godmother came to see why she cried.

"I wish I could go to the ball," Cinderella sobbed.

"Do as I say, and we'll see," said the fairy. "Get me a pumpkin from the garden."

Cinderella brought the biggest pumpkin she could find. The fairy hollowed it out, and tapped it with her wand. It became a splendid golden coach.

Then she saw six mice in a trap. She let them out, tapped them with her wand, and there stood six fine horses.

She still needed a coachman. "Would a rat do?" asked Cinderella.

"Yes, indeed," said her fairy godmother.

Cinderella brought a rat trap. The fairy chose a rat with long whiskers, and made him into a tall, bearded coachman.

Then the fairy said, "There are six lizards by the garden gate. Bring me them."

Cinderella brought them. The fairy turned them into lively, trim servants, who hopped up beside the coach.

"There, now," said the fairy. "You can go to the ball. Are you glad?"

"Yes," said Cinderella, shyly. "But can I go in these torn, old clothes?"

Then the fairy's wand really worked a wonder. Cinderella's rags became a jeweled gown of gold and silver. Her shoes turned into glass slippers, ermine-lined, and just made for dancing. She looked beautiful.

Cinderella got into her coach. Her godmother said, "Have a good time. But remember one thing. You must leave the ball by midnight. If you don't, your coach will be a pumpkin again. Your horses will be mice. Your servants will be lizards. Your glorious gown will turn back into torn old clothes."

Cinderella promised to leave before midnight, and started out for the ball.

The prince's courtiers ran to tell him an unknown, beautiful princess had arrived. He came to meet her, and led her into the ballroom. A hush fell over the guests. All eyes were on the exquisite girl. The old king stared, too, and whispered to his queen that it was years since he'd seen anyone so lovely. The ladies noted her hair and gown. They planned to buy things like Cinderella's, if they could.

The prince led her out to dance. Her dancing was a joy to see. Supper was served, but the prince's eyes never left Cinderella. She sat with her stepsisters, and gave them some fruit from a basket the prince had given her. They twittered with pride at being noticed—for they didn't recognize Cinderella at all.

As they chatted, the clock struck a quarter to twelve. Cinderella made her farewells, and left. When she got home she thanked her fairy godmother over and over. Then she asked if she might go to the ball again the next night. The prince had begged her to come. Her godmother said that she could.

Just then, her stepsisters arrived. Cinderella went, yawning, to the door, hoping they'd think she'd been asleep.

They were still exclaiming over the lovely unknown princess. "She was nicer to us than to anyone else," said the elder. "She even gave us some fruit."

Cinderella smiled, and asked, "What was her name?"

"No one knows. The prince would give anything to find out."

"How I'd love to see her. Won't you lend me a dress, so that I can go to the ball?" said Cinderella.

"What? Cindercrawler in our dresses? Never," snapped her stepsisters.

Cinderella thought it was just as well. If the mean girls had said yes, Cinderella wouldn't have known what to do.

The next night, the stepsisters went to the ball again. Cinderella went, too, even more gloriously dressed. The prince never left her side. He was so charming that she forgot the fairy's warning. She heard the clock strike twelve. Light and quick as a startled deer, she ran off. The prince couldn't catch her. But one of her slippers fell off and he picked it up tenderly. By the time she reached the gates, coach, servants, and all had gone. Nothing remained of her finery but one glass slipper.

She got home just ahead of her stepsisters. They said, "We saw the princess again. She was more beautiful than ever. But she left so suddenly she lost a glass slipper. The prince found it, and hid it next to his heart. We're sure he's in love with her."

They were right. The next day, the prince announced he would marry the girl whose foot would fit the glass slipper. Princesses, duchesses, ladies, all tried, without success. The herald brought the slipper to Cinderella's stepsisters, who tried their hardest to make the slipper fit. But they failed. Smiling, Cinderella said, "May I try too?"

Her stepsisters laughed. But the herald said, "My orders are to give a fair try to all."

Cinderella's foot fit the slipper as if it had been made for her. And, in fact, it had. The stepsisters almost fainted when Cinderella pulled the other slipper from her pocket, and put it on.

Then the fairy godmother appeared, and with a tap of her wand, Cinderella's rags were changed into the most beautiful dress you can imagine.

At last her stepsisters recognized her. They knelt at her feet, and said they were sorry for all their meanness. Cinderella hugged them, and said, "Of course I forgive you. Let's be friends from now on."

Cinderella was brought in state to the palace. There the eager prince waited. A few days later they were married, with much rejoicing.

Cinderella was just as good as she was beautiful. She brought her sisters to live in the palace, and found them good husbands as soon as she could.

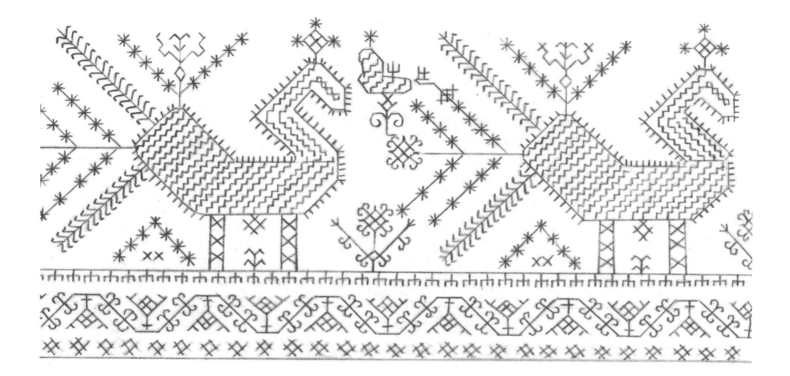

Kip, the Enchanted Cat

THERE was once a queen who had a cat. She had a husband, too, and a palace, a jewelbox, and servants, all of the best quality. But the queen treasured the cat above all.

The cat was pretty, with smoky-gray fur and sky-blue eyes. She liked to amuse the queen. She danced, chased butterflies, leapt after her tail, and was as entertaining as a cat could be. The cat led an easy life. She went everywhere with her queen, and ate royally in a cat way.

One day she had a kitten. She named it Kip.

"You're luckier than I," said the queen. "I may be queen, but I have no babies. And now you'll leave me, to care for your kitten."

"Don't cry, Majesty," said the cat, who was sensible as well as affectionate. "Crying never helps. Besides, I promise you that, as far as babies are concerned, you'll soon be as well off as I."

That night the cat ran off to the forest to find a fairy friend of hers. No one knows exactly what they talked about, but some little time later, the queen had a baby. It was a girl, gay and sweet and pretty. The queen was delighted. She called her baby Ingrid.

One day the baby caught sight of the little cat, Kip. The baby and the cat became playmates. They slept in the same crib. The princess loved Kip dearly. But, you know, a four-month-old baby is still a baby, while a little cat is quite grown up. And one evening Kip

55

went off on some cat-like errand, and she didn't come back for a long time.

Years later, Princess Ingrid was playing in the garden. She threw her ball as high as high, to see how it would come down. The ball came down and rolled under a thicket of rose bushes. Ingrid braved the thorns to reach for it.

She heard a voice say, "Hello, Ingrid."

She looked, and saw a pretty tiger-striped cat. "How do you know my name?" asked the princess.

"Don't you remember Kip?" asked the cat.

"No one I know is named Kip," said Ingrid.

"I'm Kip," purred the cat. "I used to sleep in your arms. But children have short memories, not like cats. I could go right to the room where your crib stood—our crib, it was then."

Just then Ingrid's governess called her, and came up. When she saw the cat, she cried, "Shoo, you dirty thing, go away." The cat didn't wait a moment longer. She fled to the forest before Ingrid could stop her.

When her mother came to tuck her into bed that night, Ingrid asked about the cat.

"Yes, it's quite true," said her mother. "I wish I'd seen Kip again."

Next day the sun rose early, and it was very hot. It was too hot to play, except in the shade. Ingrid led her governess toward the forest and they sat down under a big tree. Ingrid sang so softly that her governess fell asleep, as Ingrid had hoped that she would.

She slipped into the woods, calling, "Kip, Kip." At last she came to a brook, took off her shoes and socks, and went wading in the cool water. Suddenly there was a crashing noise. She looked around, and there behind her was a monster of a black-bearded giant.

He grabbed Ingrid's arm and said roughly, "Come with me." He walked so fast Ingrid had to run to keep up. Her bare feet hurt but

she did not dare ask if she could go back and put on her shoes.

Her tears made the giant furious. "I hate cry-babies," he shouted. "I'll give you something to cry for."

Thereupon he pulled out his knife, cut off her feet, and put them in his pocket. Then he strode off alone into the woods.

Ingrid fainted. When she came to, she saw she wouldn't be able to walk without her feet. The woods were silent. After a long time, Ingrid heard the sound of wheels.

"Help!" she shouted.

"Coming," cried someone. It was Kip. She was driving her own horse and carriage. Gently she picked up poor Ingrid, and put her into the carriage.

When Ingrid next opened her eyes, she was on a soft bed. Kip fed her warm milk. Her ankles didn't hurt any more, for Kip had bandaged them with an ointment made from magic healing herbs.

"You mustn't move," said Kip. "Go back to sleep while I go to find the giant and get your feet. I'll lock the door from the outside, so no one will bother you."

Kip set out in her carriage. She left it a little way from the giant's cave and quietly went to the entrance. She hid behind a rock and listened.

The giant was talking to his wife. "A disgusting cry-baby," he stormed. "I should have killed her."

"Go get her tomorrow," said his wife. "She'll make us a tasty supper."

"She's too young. They don't taste good at that age," grumbled the giant.

Kip slipped into the cave as they talked. She dumped a whole box of salt into the pot of soup that was cooking on the fire. Then Kip stole out again.

Presently the giant's wife served the soup. She and her husband drank two big bowlsful in great greedy gulps. The salt made them very thirsty.

"I must go to the brook for a drink," said the giant.

"I must, too," said his wife.

Kip ran into the cave while they were gone. In the giant's overcoat pocket she found Ingrid's feet. She took them and drove back home as fast as she could.

Ingrid was waiting for her. "Here they are," Kip said. "Don't worry. I'll have them attached to your ankles again in no time."

She bound the feet to Ingrid's ankles with a bandage of healing herbs. "You mustn't walk for a few days," Kip said. "Tomorrow, I'll drive you home. The queen will be so glad to find you safe."

The queen was, indeed, very happy to find her daughter again. As she took Ingrid from Kip's arms, she said, "How can I repay your wonderful kindness? You saved Ingrid's life. Her life is dearer to me than my own."

"Forget me for now," said Kip. "Think only of Ingrid. One day I may have a favor to ask of your majesties."

Then Kip returned to her forest home. When Ingrid heard that Kip had left, she grew very sad. She wouldn't eat, or sleep, and she would not talk of anything but Kip.

Her mother bought her new party dresses, baskets of fruit, exciting new books. But nothing would interest her.

"I don't know what to do," said the queen to the king. "I've tried everything."

"Not everything," said the king thoughtfully.

"What then?" said the queen.

"Suppose we find her a husband," said the king. "Perhaps that would interest her."

The queen agreed, and all the gayest, handsomest, best princes were brought to court. Fortunately, Ingrid smiled at the nicest of them. That smile was the first sign of many happy hours. Ingrid and the young prince were betrothed.

The day of the feast came. The bells rang out. The court rejoiced, banners flew, and the young couple were married.

After the ceremony there was a ball. Late in the evening Kip appeared. Ingrid hugged and kissed her, delighted to see her dear cat again.

"I have a favor to ask you now," said Kip.

"Yes, of course, dear Kip," said Ingrid.

"May I sleep tonight at the foot of your bed?" asked Kip.

"Is that all? Of course you may," said Ingrid.

"That's all," said Kip

That night Kip slept at the foot of Ingrid's bed. The next morning, on the cushions where Kip had slept, lay a beautiful young princess.

She quickly told her strange story. She and her mother had been enchanted by a cruel fairy. They were condemned to be cats until they had accomplished some truly amazing thing. Her mother had died without succeeding. But Kip had profited from the cruelty of the giant. She'd done something very special indeed. Now she was free, and a princess again.

Ingrid was overjoyed to have found so true a friend, and she asked Kip to come and live at court. Soon an excellent young prince was found for Kip, and there was a splendid marriage feast.

Long after, when Ingrid and Kip would sit under the trees at the edge of the forest, their grandchildren would come and ask for a story.

What story do you suppose they liked best of all to hear?

Grace and Derek

ONCE upon a time, there lived a king and queen who had one daughter. Her name was Grace, and it suited her. She was beautiful, gentle, modest, and intelligent.

Grace was the pride of the household. She spent her mornings with wise men. They shared their learning with her. In the afternoons, she worked with her mother, learning to be a queen. Her table was always set with a platter of lollypops, and twenty kinds of jam. She was a very happy girl.

Among the court ladies was the Duchess of Grudge, a hideous individual. Grudge had hot-colored hair, and a huge pimply face. She was bumpy and lumpy, and tall on one side, short on the other. She detested Grace, who seemed to grow lovelier every day. Finally, Grudge couldn't bear to see her beauty, and left court.

One day the queen took ill, and died. Grace missed her good mother. The king missed his good wife. They mourned her for a year.

At last the doctors told the king that he must have fresh air. So the king decided to go hunting. In the heat of the day, he came to a mansion. He stopped there to rest.

It was the home of the Duchess of Grudge. She came to meet the king, saying that the cellars were by far the coolest part of the house. They went down to a high cellar, where two hundred wine casks lined the walls.

"What wines have you here?" asked the king.

"Let me pour you some," said the duchess.

She pulled out a stopper. A thousand gold coins fell to the floor. "How odd," simpered Grudge.

She pulled out the stopper of the next cask. Down came a stream of more and larger gold pieces. "How very odd," Grudge grinned.

She tried the opposite row of casks. Pearls and diamonds poured all over the floor. "Well, Your Majesty, it seems there's no wine here. The casks are full of this trash, instead," said the sly Duchess of Grudge.

"Trash?" cried the king. "Do you call these riches trash?"

"You've seen nothing yet," said Grudge, who

was enjoying herself. "All my cellars are full of gold and jewels. They're yours, if you marry me."

"My dear duchess, of course I'll marry you," said the king, who worshipped money.

"There's one condition," said the duchess. "Give me charge of Grace. She must obey me absolutely."

"Agreed," said the king.

She handed him the cellar keys. Then Grudge and the king were wedded at once, in Grudge's private chapel.

The king went home, and Grace ran to meet him. "Did you enjoy the hunt?" she asked.

"I caught a great treasure," he said. "I met and married the Duchess of Grudge. You must love her, respect her, and obey her absolutely. Go dress in your best. I'm bringing her home today."

Grace always was obedient, but she could not prevent her tears as she went to her room to dress. Her nurse asked why she was crying.

"My father has married again," Grace sobbed. "My stepmother is my old enemy, the Duchess of Grudge."

"Remember you're a princess, my dear. Show your spirit. Promise me you'll never let the duchess know how you feel," said the old nurse.

It was hard. But Grace promised to show the duchess a brave face and her kindest manners.

Grace dressed in a delicate green and gold gown. She brushed out her hair, and put on a coronet of jeweled roses.

Grudge, too, was dressing with care. She wore one high shoe, so as to seem less lopsided. She dyed her hair black, and painted her face white. She squeezed into a padded dress that was supposed to make her look less lumpy. To attract attention, she sent word to the king that she wanted to be brought to his palace on the finest horse in the kingdom.

When Grace had dressed, she went walking. She stopped in a quiet wood, sighing, "At last I can cry, and not bother anyone." She wept bitterly. When she looked up, she saw coming toward her a handsome pageboy wearing green satin and a white-plumed cap.

He knelt, saying, "Princess, the king is waiting for you."

He was charming. Grace wondered why she had never seen him among the king's pages. "Have you served the king long?" she asked.

"I serve no king, my lady. I serve you, you alone. My name is Derek. I am prince of a fair kingdom. At birth I was given magical powers. They have helped me follow you everywhere, without being seen. I'll stay at your side today, disguised as a page. I may be able to help you."

"So you are the gay, clever Prince Derek that I have heard of so often. I'm glad you're my friend. I'm not so afraid of Grudge now," said Grace.

They returned to the castle. Derek had left a fine horse, beautifully saddled, in the courtyard for the princess. Grace mounted as Derek held the lead, then the king and his daughter set out to meet Grudge. In the excitement, no one noticed that Grace's horse was so beautiful that the horse that had been chosen for Grudge looked old and worn out beside it.

Grudge's carriage met them halfway. The king helped her out. She was as ugly a lump as ever, but Grace and the king embraced her and led her to the horse they had brought her. When she spied Grace's mount, she cried, "Why has that snip a finer horse than I? If you treat me that way, I'm going home."

The king quickly told Grace to give her horse to the duchess. Grace dismounted, and Grudge jumped onto the horse's back. She looked like a bundle of wet wash. Six lords held her steady, for fear she'd topple off.

With an abrupt twist the horse reared and ran off. He went so fast no one could catch him. Howling, Grudge grabbed the saddle, the horse's mane, anything she could. But she fell off, anyway, her foot caught in the stirrup.

The king was frantic. They picked up Grudge, more squashed than ever. Shoeless and hatless, she was carried to the castle and put to bed. "It's Grace's fault," she shrieked at the doctors. "She did it, to make a fool of me. She knew I'd want to ride that fancy aminal. She wanted it to run away with me. She wanted me to be killed. If the king won't agree with me, I'll leave him at once."

The king wanted peace at any price. He knew that Grudge wanted above all to be thought beautiful. So he had a flattering portrait made of her. Then he arranged a tournament. His six best knights would fight all comers to contend that Grudge was the fairest lady alive.

Many knights and lords entered the lists to deny that Grudge was the queen of beauty. Seated in a gold pavilion, Grudge watched every joust, and beamed for joy as the king's knights won every time. The lords had eyes only for Grace, who stood behind her step-mother. Silly Grudge was sure they were staring at her.

The last contestant on the list was a young knight who carried a portrait in a diamond box. He announced that Grudge was the ugliest lady alive, and that the lady whose portrait he carried was the most fair. He rode against six knights at once, and knocked them from their horses. Six more took their place, then six more, until he had beaten twenty-four champions.

To console the defeated knights he showed them the picture in his box. It was of Grace. He bowed low to her, and quit the field without giving his name. But Grace knew in her heart that it must be Derek.

Grudge almost choked with wrath. "How dare Grace compete with my beauty? I'll fix her," she raged.

Late that night, Grudge's soldiers took Grace deep into a forest full of wild beasts. They left her there, alone and helpless.

Grace went stumbling through the dark. She fell, sobbing, and cried, "Derek, where are you? Have you, too, forgotten me?"

As she spoke, a marvelous thing happened. Clusters of lighted candles sprang up on every branch. Ahead, Grace saw a glittering crystal palace.

Twigs crackled near by. Afraid, expecting wolves or bears, she looked around, and there was Derek, a gay, glad sight. "Don't be afraid, my lady," he said. "I love you so. Come to the fairy palace. My mother and sisters are there, and they love you, too."

Delightful music drifted across the air as they neared the palace. The queen and her daughters welcomed Grace lovingly. They showed her a room with rock crystal walls. Grace stared, amazed, for the walls were engraved with her own life story, and even showed her entrance into the palace.

"I want to remember everything about you, forever," explained Derek.

Grace did not know what to answer. The queen said kindly, "You must be hungry and weary, after your adventure. Come to dinner."

After a good meal, Grace was tired. She was shown to her room. Thirty exquisite young girls helped her into bed, and she fell asleep to the sound of their soft music.

When she woke, they showed her rows of dresses, and boxes filled with tiaras, jewels, ribbons, slippers—everything she could want, all her size and exactly to her taste.

She found Derek and said, "I must thank you. You've saved me and taken such good care of me. But what shall I do next? My father must be worrying. And I'm afraid Grudge will never give me any peace."

"You're safe here," he said. "Why leave? Say you'll marry me, and forget that mean old hag, Grudge."

"If I could do as I liked, I'd stay," said Grace. "But I can't let my father think me dead. My duty is to him. I must do what's right, no matter what."

Derek tried hard to change her mind, but she refused. Finally, Derek made Grace invisible so that she could enter the castle unseen. She went straight to her father's room. At first he thought her a ghost. Then Grace explained that Grudge had hoped to kill her, but that she had somehow survived and made her way home again. She asked the king to send her to a far corner of the country, where Grudge might leave her in peace.

The king was dismayed by Grudge's cruelty. Had he been a strong, wise man, he'd have put Grudge in her place. But he was under his new wife's thumb. He never got truly angry with her. Instead of scolding Grudge, he chatted with Grace, and ordered a fine supper for them both.

Grudge's servants saw Grace, and told Grudge that Grace was back, alive. When the king went to bed, Grudge went into action.

She had Grace dragged to a prison cell. She gave her a ragged old dress and took away her fine clothes. For a mattress, she threw in a handful of straw.

Grace thought sadly of the fairy palace that she had left. She had been hard on Derek. She didn't dare call on him for help.

Grudge sent for her fairy friend, who was just as nasty as Grudge herself. "There's a girl who's rude to me," Grudge told the fairy. "Let's make her wretched. We'll find ugly, impossible tasks for her to do. We'll give her no rest."

The fairy loved a chance to show off her nasty imagination. "Try this," she said.

She gave Grudge a huge wad of tangled thread, so fine that it broke if you looked at it hard enough.

Grudge took the wad of thread to her prisoner. "Here's a job for you," she said. "Untangle this thread, and wind it up properly, before dark. If you break it, even once, you'll be sorry."

Grudge left, locking the door behind her. Grace tried to untangle the thread, but it broke into knots of fluff, no matter what she did.

She put it down, and sighed, "Let Grudge kill me, then. I can't manage this thread. Derek, if you can't help me now, at least come to say good-by, forever."

Derek came right through the locked door with no trouble at all. "Here I am, my lady," he said. "It seems you only want to see me when you're in trouble." He tapped his wand. The thread untangled, and wound itself into a perfectly neat ball.

"Don't be cross," said Grace. "I'm miserable enough already."

"Free yourself from misery, my lady," begged Derek. "Come away, and marry me. Why ever not?"

"What if you don't truly love me?" said Grace. "We've only known each other a short time. Can I trust your love?"

Derek tried to hide his hurt feelings, and bowed low as he said good-by.

Grudge could hardly wait till it was dark. She unlocked the door, smiling, sure that Grace would have failed in her task.

When Grace gave her the neat ball of thread she was exceedingly angry. She couldn't complain about the thread, except to say that it was soiled. So she said that Grace was a dirty girl, and she slapped her cheeks black and blue.

Grudge sent for the nasty fairy again. "Do better this time. Invent something very hard, and much more unpleasant," she said.

The fairy came back with a bag as big as two men. It was full of feathers. There were thousands of feathers from birds of every kind —blue jay and bluebird, cardinal and tanager, starling, raven, and crow—every bird you've ever seen or heard of.

Grudge dumped the feathers into Grace's cell. "Separate them into little packets, one packet for each kind of bird," she said. "Make no mistake. I want them all arranged by nightfall, or you'll be sorry."

Grace picked up a handful. No one could tell one bird's feathers from another. Even the birds they belonged to would have been confused.

"This is hopeless," thought Grace. "I shan't call Derek. If he really cared, he'd be here by now."

"I am here, my lady," he said, as he appeared. Three taps of his wand, and all the feathers were sorted in tidy piles.

"My lord, I owe you everything," exclaimed Grace. "I'll never forget your goodness to me."

He vanished as Grudge opened the door. Grudge was beside herself with anger to see the feathers sorted, and she hit Grace as hard as she could.

Once again Grudge summoned the nasty fairy. The fairy said, "Try her with this box. If she opens it, she'll never get it shut again. Send her somewhere with it. She's sure to be curious and open it. Then you'll have every right to punish her as you please."

Grudge was a clever schemer. She gave Grace the box, saying, "Take this to my mansion. Put it on the drawing-room table. The things in it are too precious for you to see. I forbid you to open it, on pain of death."

Grace set off, dressed in her rags. Those who saw her thought she must be an angel in disguise, she was so beautiful.

After many miles, she stopped to rest. The box was on her knees. "I wonder what's in here?" she said. "Why not look? I shan't touch anything. Just one peek won't hurt."

She opened the box, and out leapt a crowd of tiny creatures. There were lords and ladies, cooks and musicians, and there were violins, flutes, tables, dishes, silverware, all sorts of things, and the biggest was no bigger than your finger.

The musicians began to play. The lords and ladies danced. The cooks cooked. The lords and ladies sat at table and ate. Their antics charmed Grace.

But when she wanted to put them back into the box, they scattered and hid. Not one was to be seen.

"Now I'm really in trouble," cried Grace. "I've done wrong, out of stupid curiosity. Whatever happens now, it will truly be my own fault. Derek, if you still care for such a silly girl, save me now."

He appeared at once. "Wicked as Grudge is," Derek said, "I'm grateful to her for one thing. Her mean tricks make you call for me."

He tapped the box with his wand. Tiny creatures ran from all sides and jumped into the box. Soon the box was exactly as it had been before.

Derek waved his wand, and his chariot appeared. He quickly drove Grace to Grudge's mansion, and they knocked at the gate.

Grace asked to go to the drawing room, where Grudge had told her to leave the box.

The caretaker laughed. "Who ever heard of a dirty peasant in a queen's drawing room? Wooden shoes don't come walking on these floors," he said.

Grace asked for a written message to tell Grudge that he wouldn't let her in. The caretaker wrote it for her. Derek was waiting, and they drove back to the palace.

Grudge hid her disgust at the sight of Grace, for she had another plan ready. The wicked queen had had a big pit dug in the garden. It was covered by a rock.

That evening, Grudge went walking with her maids and Grace. When they came to the rock, Grudge said, "I hear there's treasure hidden under this rock. Lift it, and let's see."

The maids pushed the rock up. When they had lifted it high enough, Grudge shoved Grace into the pit. Then she called the maids away, and the rock fell back into place.

In the dark, underground, Grace had no hope. "I am buried alive," she thought. "I will surely

die. Derek, this is my punishment for not trusting your love."

Trying not to cry, she looked around. A door appeared in the side of the pit and began to open. Through it, Grace could see daylight, and a garden of fruits and flowers, fountains and summer-houses. She went through the door.

Before her lay a long avenue of trees. It led her, as if in a dream, to the crystal fairy palace.

Derek, his mother, and his sisters, came to meet her. Grace stretched out her arms to them all. "Derek," she said, shyly, "I've been unkind to you. Please forgive me. If you care for such a silly girl, I'll marry you now."

They were married at once, in the fairy garden. The ceremony was performed with every perfection, to the sound of fountains and fairy music.

Urashima and the Turtle

THERE was once a young fisherman, the son of sons of fishermen. He loved the sea, the crash of the waves and the shifting tides. He lived at the shore. He loved to watch the sea by night and by day, winter and summer, stormy and fair.

His name was Urashima. At dawn he went out in his boat. He came home again at dusk. Sometimes the fishing was good, sometimes it was poor. If he had had his way he would never have kept the fish he caught. He'd have thrown them back in the water to live, for he thought the fish were beautiful. Their skins flashed silver. They were delicately made, and strong.

Late one afternoon Urashima felt a tug at his line. He reeled in. He expected to see the shimmer of a sea bass. Instead he saw a turtle.

Urashima smiled, and threw the turtle back in the water. "I'd sooner go hungry tonight than kill a young turtle," he said. Turtles live long, long lives, and this one was young.

The turtle hit the water in a wide splash of foam. From the spray sprung a girl more beautiful than the day and the night together. She came to sit at Urashima's side.

She said, "I am the Sea King's daughter. We live at the bottom of the sea. Father let me change into a turtle, to test your good heart. Indeed you are good, and kind. Will you come and share my dragon palace in the kingdom of green waves?"

67

Urashima saw only her great beauty. He wanted to be with her always.

"Yes," he said. They each of them took an oar. They rowed the boat beneath the waves, to the bottom of the sea. Crystalline fish with golden crests swam to escort them.

Before the sun had set, they reached the palace. It was made of coral and pearl. It glimmered as if all the world's jewels were shining underwater in a soft wash of moonlight.

Velvet-finned little dragons obeyed their every wish in that palace. They fed on the delicacies that the sea gives only to those who love her.

In the perfect quiet of that place Urashima lived four years with his princess. Day and night, the sea anemones danced, light, soundless, and slow, in the luminous water.

They were very happy until one day, Urashima saw a young turtle. It reminded him of the day when he'd come under the sea. He thought of his village and of his family.

The princess knew at once that he was thinking of home.

"You miss the earth and your people," she said. "If you stay here, you'll hate me for keeping you. If you go now, you may come back. Take this pearl box, tied with green ribbon. Keep it safe. It will bring you here when you're ready. But keep the ribbon tied. If the bow comes undone, and the box is opened, you'll never return."

Urashima got into his boat and the princess thrust it up through the waves. Soon he was on top of the water, sailing for home. There stood his hill and his cherry trees. There lay the sand where he'd built castles as a boy.

Memory made his heart pound. He hurried up a path he knew well.

At first he thought nothing had changed. The sky shone blue, crickets chirped, rocks stood out of the sand, as they always had.

But when he came to where his house had been, he felt lost. The house was gone. Even the tree that had shadowed it was gone.

He went on. All the houses were different. Children stared at him. What had happened in the four years he was under the sea?

He saw an old man sitting in the sun, and he went to talk to him.

"Beg pardon, sir, can you tell me how to find Urashima's house?" he asked.

"Urashima?" said the old man, puzzled. "It's an odd name. I never heard it but once before. That was in my great-grandfather's story of a boy who was drowned. His brothers, their sons, and their sons' sons lived hereabouts. But the family died out, long before my time. It's a sad little tale, isn't it, stranger? A young man went fishing, four hundred years ago, and disappeared. They never found even a stick from his boat. The sea simply swallowed him up," said the old man.

Fatherless, motherless, brotherless, homeless, Urashima was a stranger in his own village.

The old man pointed with his cane. "You might find his tombstone in the old cemetery," he said, "down that way."

Slowly, Urashima went to the cemetery. There, beside his parents' tombstones, and his brothers', was his own name, cut in a worn old stone.

Now Urashima understood. There was nothing for him in this village. Here on earth, he had been dead and gone for four hundred years. He must return at once to his beloved princess.

He still had the pearl box, tied with green ribbon. He knew he mustn't lose it. He knew he should hurry, but he felt tired and discouraged.

He went back to the beach, slowly. He sat

to rest on the sand, with the box on his knees. He wondered how he could return to the palace. Brooding, without thinking, he untied the ribbon around the box.

Absent-mindedly, slowly, he opened the box. A white mist drifted up and hung an instant on the air. It had the shape, cloud-soft, of his dear princess.

Urashima held out his arms but the mist disappeared on a sea breeze. He ran after it, but it had gone.

At the water's edge he stopped. He felt so old. His back bent. His hands shook. His hair whitened and fell. His muscles failed and vanished. He withered away, from top to toe.

Soon on the white beach lay a skeleton fit for a grave dug four hundred years before.

When the moon stood above the pine trees, it shone on the waves that gather and break, gather and break, over and over, forever. It shone on a little empty pearl box, and a green ribbon fluttering in the wind.

Thumbkin

Once, a woodsman and his wife had seven boys. There were ten-year-old twins, nine-year-old twins, eight-year-old twins, and one single seven-year-old. The seven-year-old was very small and very quiet. At birth, he'd been no bigger than your thumb, and so he was named Thumbkin.

Thumbkin was the cleverest of the boys. His family thought he was stupid, for he didn't talk much. But he surely knew how to listen.

The woodsman was very poor, and the family often went hungry. One year, they were hungry all the time, for there was famine.

When the boys were abed, the worried woodsman spoke to his wife. "What shall we do?" he asked. "We love our boys. We cannot watch them die of hunger. Tomorrow we must lead them far into the forest, and lose them."

"We can't. It's too cruel," cried his wife. She knew they had no food, but she dearly loved her boys.

"In the forest, a miracle might save them," said the woodsman. "At home, they'll surely starve."

His wife wept, but she had to agree.

Thumbkin had heard every word, for he was a most noticing child, and he quickly made a plan. He slipped outside, and packed his pockets full of shiny pebbles. Then he went to bed.

Next morning, the woodsman took the boys deep into the woods. While he chopped wood, the boys gathered twigs. Little by little, the woodsman moved away. Soon he couldn't see the boys. He returned home, alone.

When the boys saw their father had gone, they were afraid. But Thumbkin had taken care to drop pebbles along the way into the woods. They would lead him back home. So he said to his brothers, "Don't cry. Follow me, and we'll be home in no time."

With Thumbkin leading them, the seven boys trooped home. They stood outside the door, afraid to go in.

They didn't know that the woodsman had had a surprise while they were away. A man who had owed him money for a long time had at last paid it back, and his wife had been able to buy lots of food.

As the hungry pair sat down to eat, the wife began to weep. "I wish our boys were here. I'd give them such a good dinner."

The boys heard her. "Here we are, Mother!" they shouted. They all piled into the house, and sat down to a good supper.

Until the food was gone, the family was merry together. But when the cupboard was bare, the woodcutter decided that he would have to lose his boys again.

He told his wife that he would take the boys deep into the forest that day. Once again, Thumbkin heard him. He tried to slip out and get pebbles. But the doors were locked.

Next day, as they left the house, their mother gave them some bread for lunch. Thumbkin left a trail of bread crumbs to lead them home.

They went into the deepest part of the woods. While they were busy working, their father left them alone. Thumbkin wasn't worried, for he expected the bread crumbs would lead them home. But when he looked, he found not a crumb. The birds had eaten them all.

The lost boys walked and walked. Night fell, and the wind howled. The boys shook in their shoes. It began to rain, a cold, cold rain. Thumbkin climbed a tree to see what he could see. Far to the left, he saw a light. He got down, and led his brothers to the left.

Near the edge of the forest they found a lighted house. A woman answered Thumbkin's knock at the door, and Thumbkin said, "Madam, we boys are lost. Can you keep us with you for tonight?"

"You poor creatures!" cried the woman. "Don't you know this is the home of an ogre who eats boys?"

The boys stood bunched together at the door. "What can we do?" said Thumbkin. "If you don't let us in, wolves will surely eat us. Maybe your husband will be kinder than the wolves."

"Very well," said the ogre s wife. "Come and get warm at the fire."

As they were drying out their wet clothes there was a great banging at the door. It was the ogre! His wife quickly pushed the boys under the bed, and let the ogre in.

He sat right down at the table and started to eat. Then he began to sniff. "I smell live meat," he said.

"I've been skinning a goat," said his wife.

"I smell *live* meat," roared the ogre. "You can't fool me."

He went straight to the bed, and looked underneath it. He dragged out the boys one by one. "Good," he shouted. "Seven nice tender boys. They'll make a nice dessert for my dinner party this week."

The boys got on their knees and begged for mercy, but the ogre merely licked his lips. He sharpened his long knife and he picked up a boy. He was just about to spear him, when his wife said, "There's no need to do it tonight. There'll be plenty of time tomorrow."

"*Quiet!*" roared the ogre.

Quickly, his wife said, "But they'll spoil before you can eat them. The pantry's full of meat already."

"You're right," said the ogre, dropping the boy. "Feed them well, and put them to bed. We'll fatten them up for a day or so."

The good wife was glad of the chance to feed the boys. Afterwards she took them to the room where her own daughters slept. There were seven of these young ogresses. They all slept in one big bed, each with a gold crown on her head. They all had tiny eyes, sharp noses, and enormous mouths full of long, pointed teeth. There was another big bed in their room. The ogre's wife put the boys in the second bed.

Thumbkin noticed the seven crowns on the heads of the seven ogresses. He thought,

"Suppose the ogre changes his mind and decides to kill us tonight?"

Thumbkin took the boys' caps, and crept across the room. He exchanged the caps for the ogresses' crowns. He put the crowns on his and his brothers' heads. Then he waited.

He had been wise. The ogre awoke, late that night, sorry that he hadn't yet made meat out of the boys. Knife in hand, he hurried to the children's bedroom. He reached out in the dark, and felt a crowned head. He went to the other side of the room, shaking his head and saying, "I almost got mixed up, and killed my own nice ogresses."

He came to the other bed and felt a head wearing a cap. "There they are," he said. Quickly and neatly, he cut the throats of the seven ogresses. Then, smiling with satisfaction, he went back to bed and slept.

When Thumbkin heard the ogre snore, he woke his brothers. Quickly they dressed, then they tiptoed out and ran and ran.

Next morning, the ogre wanted to put the fresh meat in the pantry. He went to the children's room, and there were the ogresses, dead as could be. "It's a trick," he howled. "They'll pay for this!"

He jammed on his seven-league boots, and ran out. He covered the countryside in a few strides and soon came to the road the boys had taken. They were close to their father's home when they saw the ogre coming. He was stepping from hill to hill, and striding across broad rivers as if they were the smallest of puddles.

Thumbkin spied a hollow rock and quickly got his brothers in under it, then followed them. Along came the ogre, out of breath. Seven-league boots go fast, but they tire out the man who wears them, just as if he'd run the whole distance without their help. The ogre stopped to rest.

As luck would have it, he lay down right next to the rock where Thumbkin and his brothers were hidden. He fell fast asleep.

Thumbkin said, "Don't worry. Run home, while he's asleep. I'll see you later." The boys ran off and arrived home in no time.

Meanwhile, Thumbkin softly tugged off the ogre's seven-league boots, and put them on himself. They were far too big, of course. But seven-league boots shrink, or grow, to fit their wearer perfectly. In a minute, they fit Thumbkin.

He strode to the ogre's house, and said to the ogre's wife, "Thieves have captured your husband, and they will kill him if he doesn't give them all his money. He asked me to fetch all his wealth, every bit. He doesn't want to die."

The ogre's wife gave Thumbkin bundles of bills and sacks of gold. Thumbkin hurried home to his family with all that wealth on his back. Without his seven-league boots the ogre could not find the brothers, so he quietly went home. It took him a very long time.

As you may imagine, the family was filled with pride for the youngest son. "Thumbkin is small," said his mother, "but he is not stupid."

The Wild Swans

ONCE there lived a king who had eleven sons, and one daughter, named Lisa. He loved them all well, and played with them often. They were lucky children.

But their happiness didn't last. Their father married a queen who hated children. As soon as she could, she sent Lisa to live with a farmer. She told lies about the boys, and blamed them for everything, until soon the king didn't care for his sons at all.

One day the queen sent for the boys. She said, "Boys you are, but birds you'll be. Fly away, wretched creatures."

The boys turned into eleven splendid white swans. They opened their great wings and flew out of the window with a strange, sad cry. Up they went, cloud-high, far and far.

Lisa wasn't allowed out of the farmhouse. She had no toys or friends. Year after year went by, and she had nothing to do but look out the window, and sing to the roses.

She read in the prayer-book, and said, "Book, what is as good as you?"

The wind and the book sang, "Lisa is as good."

And it was true.

When Lisa was fifteen, the king wanted to see his daughter again. The queen still hated Lisa's goodness and beauty. But she knew that the king wanted to see the child once more. She would have turned her into a swan, if she had dared.

Instead, she mixed a muddy, stinking stain. She smeared Lisa's face, arms, and hair with it. Then she brought Lisa to the king. When he saw the smelly, splotchy girl, he said, "She's no daughter of mine."

The queen threw Lisa out.

Lisa wandered through a forest, thinking of her brothers. She didn't know they were swans. She hoped to find them somehow. Night came. Lisa lay down to sleep, whispering a prayer. Fireflies hung like jewels on the bushes, sparkling in the dusky air.

When Lisa woke, the sun was up. Birds sang. She found a pond and drank. When she saw the reflection of her face and arms, she cried out in horror. She scrubbed herself hard until she was clean again.

Now she was hungry. She knew the earth is full of good things to eat if only one looks. She found an apple tree, and had a good breakfast.

Lisa walked on through the quiet forest. By nightfall she was tired. At the forest's far edge she lay down, and slept deep.

Lisa waked with the sun. A woman came by with a bucket of raspberries. She gave some to Lisa.

"Please, have you seen eleven princes anywhere?" asked Lisa.

"No," said the woman. "But I've seen eleven crowned swans in the river near here."

She led Lisa to a high river bank. From it they could see the sea in the distance. The woman left Lisa there. Lisa wondered where to look first. Bits of glass and stone edged the river. The water had worn them smooth.

"The river never stops," said Lisa to herself. "With patience, it changes everything it touches. I'll be patient as a river. I'll look forever. I'll find my brothers."

She went down the river, toward the sea.

Toward sunset she found eleven swan plumes. High and far overhead she saw a gleaming white streak that came closer as she watched. Soon she could make out the broad wing-sweep of eleven swans.

She hid in a clump of bushes. The swans settled on the river bank with a clatter of their big wings. The moment the sun set beyond the sea the swans rose up from their feathers, and changed into men. They were Lisa's eleven brothers.

She came to them with a happy cry. They hugged her, and cried for joy. What a good talk they had, all of them together once again!

They told each other all their adventures.

"We're swans by day," the eldest brother told her. "At sundown we become men. We have to be on solid ground at dark. If we were flying at the moment of change, we'd fall down to earth."

"We don't live here all the time," the next brother went on. "Only once a year, for eleven days, we are allowed to visit our own land. This is the happiest visit ever, for we've found you, Lisa."

"Where do you live the rest of the year?" Lisa asked.

"Beyond the sea. We need two days to fly across. We'd never manage the trip if it weren't for a rock that lies halfway across the sea. It's just big enough for us to spend the night on. In bad weather we have to huddle close together. But it's been safe, so far."

"When do your eleven days end?" asked Lisa.

"In two days," said the eldest. "I wish you'd come with us."

"If only you could keep your own bodies forever," said Lisa.

Lisa woke the next day to the beating of wings. Her brothers, swans once more, were flying off for the day. The youngest stayed behind. He couldn't talk, but he and Lisa looked at the world, and were together.

At evening the others came back. The sun set. They became men again.

"Little sister," said the eldest, "how brave are you? Tomorrow we leave here. Will you let us fly you over the sea?"

"Yes," said Lisa, "gladly."

All night they worked. They wove a net of boughs and vines. At daybreak the brothers became swans again. Lisa lay in the net. The swans took its edges in their beaks, and flew off with it.

The youngest swan flew overhead to keep the sun out of Lisa's eyes. She slept a while. When she woke, she ate the berries she'd brought. There was nothing but water below, wherever Lisa looked.

The swans flew slower than usual, with Lisa to carry. By late afternoon Lisa was worried. She couldn't see the rock they must reach before dark. A stormy wind blew up. Lightning flashed. The sun was at the sky's very rim, and still Lisa saw no rock. She whispered a prayer for the brothers and for herself, sure that they were lost. But just as the sun set, she saw the rock beneath, and as darkness fell, her feet touched solid ground.

A minute later, her brothers were standing tall around her, with linked arms. The rock was just big enough to hold them. A storm raged, but the twelve held tight, and sang. The night went fast, because they were brave.

By dawn the storm had ended. The air was clean and fresh. With Lisa in her net once more, the swans flew on. At noon Lisa saw the shores of a country quite like her own. At sunset the swans alighted near a wood.

At once they turned into men, and took Lisa to a green grotto where she could sleep.

"I wonder what you'll dream tonight?" said the youngest brother.

"I hope I dream how to save you," she answered.

Lisa did dream. In her dream she met a woman. The woman was queenly, yet somehow she seemed like the woman who had given Lisa the raspberries in the wood, and had told her about the eleven crowned swans.

"You can save your brothers," said the woman. "Have you courage and patience? If you do try to save them, no one will understand you. You'll be tired, alone, and afraid. Here's what must be done. Near this grotto grow many nettles. They burn and sting like fire if you touch them. You must pick every last one. Only these nettles, or nettles that grow in cemeteries, will do this work.

"Pick them, crush them, and spin them into a green thread. Then knit eleven coats. The moment you put the coats on your brothers, they'll be free from their spell.

"The hardest part is this: from start to finish, you must work without speaking. If you say one word, it will be like plunging a knife into your brothers' hearts. They will die. Remember!"

Lisa awoke and she began gathering nettles at once. They burned and stung and blistered her hands until they were red and sore. But she kept on. She was determined to free her brothers. She kept crushing the nettles, and spinning the green thread, all that day.

When her brothers came that night, they saw her hard at her work. She shook her head, a finger on her lips. They knew then that she was trying to help them.

She was in such a hurry she worked all night. Next day, she kept on working. She had made one coat, and part of a second, when suddenly she heard the sound of hunters'

horns. She bundled the nettles up, and ran into the grotto. Hunting dogs barked nearer, and nearer, and burst into the grotto.

Huntsmen followed them. The handsomest hunter was the king of that country.

"How did you get here, lovely child?" he asked.

She shook her head. She longed to speak, but she knew that one word would kill the swans.

"Come with me," said the king. "If you're as good as you are lovely, I'll make you my queen." He set her before him on his horse. She wept, but he held her firm on his horse.

"It's for your own good, little one," said the kind king. "Don't cry. I'll make you happy."

Lisa did not dare speak. The king led her into the palace. His maids cared for Lisa, and dressed her royally. She was so perfectly lovely that everyone who saw her loved her.

Only the archbishop shook his head and muttered, "She's from the wild-wood. She's too beautiful. She must be a witch." No one listened to him.

The king sat next to her at dinner. They watched a ballet. They walked through gardens where fountains danced in the flower-scented air. But Lisa could think only of her brothers, and her nettles, and she wept.

Then the king showed her a room next to his own. He'd had it made just for her. It was hung and painted to look just like the green grotto where he had found her. On the ground was the bundle of nettles and the coats that she had knitted, just as she had left them when the hunters came.

"See, little one," said the king, "this is to remind you of the hardships you've left behind. I hope to make you happier here."

The sight of the nettles made Lisa feel better. She smiled, and kissed the good king's

hand. He believed it was a sign of love. He ordered the bells to be rung to announce his engagement.

The archbishop was still muttering, but no one paid him heed, and next day Lisa married the king. She couldn't say a word, but love for the king's kind heart shone in her eyes. She was crowned his queen, with much rejoicing.

Lisa longed to confide in her husband, but she knew that she could not. Each night, secretly, she slipped from her bed and knitted the coats for her brothers. When she'd made seven coats, she had no more nettles.

"I must go to the cemetery," she remembered. "Only cemetery nettles will do." Though she was afraid, she went to the cemetery. The moon made weird shadows across the graves.

Lisa was sure witches hid in those shadows, and she was frightened. But she said a prayer, and bravely gathered the nettles. Then she hurried back as quietly as she had left.

She thought no one knew she'd been out. But the sly, jealous archbishop had seen her. Now he was sure Lisa was a witch. He told the king.

At first the king would not believe him.

"Why don't you watch her," sneered the jealous archbishop. "See if she goes there again."

Doubt touched the king's heart. He hated to spy. But he hoped he'd be able to tell the archbishop how silly he was. For several nights he only pretended to be asleep. He saw Lisa get up and go to her little grotto room.

Her work was almost done. Ten coats were ready. But she had no more nettles. She would have to go once more to the cemetery. The idea terrified her, but she set her will to it, for her brothers' sake.

That night when Lisa went to the cemetery, the king and the archbishop were following. They saw the witches gathered in the shadows.

Hans went outside.

That night he wanted to sleep in his old room that he had shared with the other apprentices.

"You're too dirty," they said. "Go to the chicken coop." So Hans went to sleep in the chicken coop, with the chickens.

On the third morning a gold carriage, drawn by six huge horses, stopped at the mill. A seventh horse was on a lead beside the carriage. A beautiful princess stepped out.

"Miller!" she called.

The old man ran out, bowing and panting. He'd never seen such richness.

"I want your youngest apprentice, wonderful Hans who worked seven years for me," said the princess.

"He's in the chicken coop, Your Highness," said the amazed old man.

"Fetch him, then," said the princess.

Cat-servants had already gone to the chicken coop. They'd brought a dozen buckets of water, and they scrubbed Hans until he was shiny clean. Then they dressed him in princely clothes. His shoes had silver buckles. His tie was embroidered in gold. He was handsome as a king.

The princess smiled when she saw him. "Miller," she said, "this horse is for you, from Hans." She gave the bridle of the seventh horse to the miller.

"I never thought I'd ever see so fine a horse," said the miller. "It is certainly Hans who inherits the mill."

"Keep your mill, and the horse, too," said the princess.

She took Hans by the arm, and led him to her carriage. Then away they went.

They stopped where Hans had built the pretty silver house. It had become a great, beautiful castle. Hans and the princess were married. They were so rich Hans never had to work again, except for fun.

Little Red Riding Hood

Once upon a time there was a little girl who was as pretty as could be. Her mother and her grandmother loved her very much. Her grandmother made her a red hood, and it looked so becoming on the little girl that everyone called her Little Red Riding Hood.

One day her mother baked a batch of cookies. "Red Riding Hood," she said, "Grandmother is sick. Will you take her these cookies, and a pot of fresh butter?"

Red Riding Hood set out at once. Her grandmother lived in the next village, beyond the woods.

As she was going through the woods, she met a wolf. The wolf would have liked to eat her, but he didn't dare, because there were woodsmen working nearby. He thought of a plan.

"Where are you going, my dear?" asked the wolf.

"To see my grandmother," said Red Riding Hood. "I have cookies, and a pot of fresh butter for her."

"Have you far to go?" asked the wolf.

"Yes," said Red Riding Hood. "Her house is way over there, the first one past the woods."

"I'll go see her, too," said the wolf. "I'll take this path, and you take the other path. We'll see who gets there first."

The wolf ran fast, and he took a short cut. Red Riding Hood took the long way. She picked some flowers. She sang some songs. She chased some butterflies. The wolf came to the grandmother's door while Red Riding Hood was still far away. He knocked twice.

"Who's there?" called Grandmother.

"It's Red Riding Hood," said the wolf, in a Red-Riding-Hood voice. "I've brought you some cookies, and a pot of fresh butter."

Grandmother was in bed, for she was sick. "Open the door and come in," she called.

The wolf came in. He hadn't eaten for three days, and he was very hungry. He ate the grandmother very quickly. Then he wrapped himself in Grandmother's shawl. He climbed into Grandmother's bed. Soon, Red Riding Hood came knocking at the door.

"Who's there?" called the wolf, in a grandmotherly voice.

He sounded hoarse, but Red Riding Hood thought that Grandmother must have a bad cold. "It's Red Riding Hood," she said. "I've brought you some cookies, and a pot of fresh butter."

"Open the door and come in," said the wolf, as sweetly as he could.

The wolf pulled the covers up to his ears. "Put your basket on the table and come here to me," said the wolf.

Red Riding Hood came closer. She said, "Grandmother, what long arms you have."

"The better to hug you with, my dear," said the wolf.

She said, "Grandmother, what big ears you have."

"The better to hear you with, my dear," said the wolf.

She said, "Grandmother, what big eyes you have."

"The better to see you with, my dear," said the wolf.

She said, "Grandmother, what big teeth you have."

"The better to eat you with," said the wolf. And eat her he did.

But he howled so loud, in his true wolf voice, that a woodsman heard him.

The woodsman ran in with his ax. He hacked hard at the wolf, and the wolf split right down the middle.

Out hopped Red Riding Hood, as good as new. Out stepped her grandmother, looking surprised.

They put the wolf in the garbage, and that was the end of him. Then they invited the woodsman to sit down. There were plenty of buttered cookies for the three of them. They had a very good time.

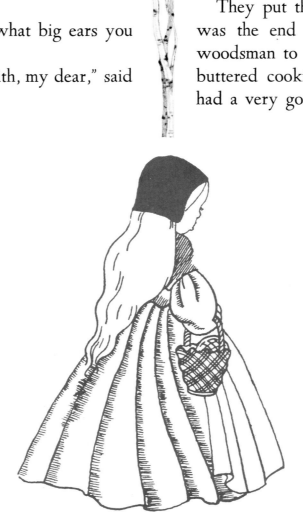

The White Deer

ONCE upon a time lived a king and queen who ruled happily. Their only sorrow was that they had no children.

One day, the queen went walking alone. She sat by a forest well to rest. "I wish I had a child," she cried for the hundreth time.

The waters of the well foamed and bubbled, and up came a large shrimp. It said, "Queen, your wish will come true. Will you let a mere shrimp lead you to a fairy palace that no mortal eye can find?"

The queen said, "I'll gladly go. But I can't swim backwards underwater, as shrimp do."

The shrimp laughed, and turned into a handsome old lady. She wasn't even damp as she stepped out of the water. She wore a white dress, crimson lined, and her gray hair was prettily decorated with green ribbons.

The queen followed her into dense woods. A fairy path opened out as they walked. Orange trees made a flowery roof. Violets carpeted the ground.

At last they came to a palace made entirely of diamonds, from roof-tree to cellar. Its doors opened, and six magnificent fairies brought out gifts to the queen. Each fairy gave her a jeweled flower, so that she had a bouquet with a carnation, a rose, a tulip, an anemone, a pink, and a pomegranate flower.

"Majesty," they said, "few mortals may come here. Your faithful wish for a child has won our hearts. You'll have a child, named Faith. When she is born, take the jeweled bouquet we've given you. Call the name of each flower. We will appear, and give Faith the best of our gifts."

The queen was beside herself with joy. She thanked the fairies over and over again, giving special thanks to the Well Fairy. Then she went home joyously.

After a time, she had a baby girl, and she named her Faith. She took out the bouquet and named the flowers. At once the air was full of fairies. They were followed by their servants, little dwarfs who carried armloads of presents.

There were shirts and diapers and gowns and blankets and booties and bonnets. Everything was ruffled, embroidered, tasseled, monogrammed, and edged in lace. Anyone could see that no mere mortal had made such exquisite things.

The fairies played with the baby a while. Then they got to work. They gave her great gifts: goodness, intelligence, perfect beauty, good luck, and good health.

As the queen thanked the fairies, the door slammed open and a great shrimp came in. "Forgot me, didn't you!" she cried. "You owe this happy day to me. I accuse you of ingratitude. I'm disguised as a shrimp, for your thanks to me goes backwards, like a shrimp does."

The queen was wretched. Humbly she begged pardon. "The bouquet confused me. Truly I am most grateful to you. I made a terrible mistake," she said.

The fairies joined in. "Dear Sister Well, do stop being a shrimp. Show us your charming form. Forget a mortal's mistake. She meant no harm to your beloved self."

"Very well," said Well Fairy, who liked to be flattered. "I'll let the child live. But I warn you, if she sees daylight before she's fifteen, something terrible will happen. If you let her see the sun, beware!" With that, she vanished.

"What am I to do?" cried the queen.

The fairies put their heads together and thought. Then they said, "We'll build you a windowless, doorless palace with an underground entry. The princess will be safe in it until she's fifteen."

Three taps of all their wands built the palace. Its inside walls were jeweled with patterns of birds and flowers. There was no daylight anywhere, but candles made it bright. One wing of the palace was set aside for learned men, who were to be Faith's teachers. As the

years passed, her ready mind surprised her teachers. She loved to learn.

Faith also had gaiety and good looks that delighted everyone.

Often the fairies came to see her. Tulip, especially, loved Faith. She often reminded the queen, "Well Fairy has a long memory. We must keep Faith out of daylight until she's fifteen." The queen promised to be careful.

When Faith was fourteen and a half, her portrait was painted. It was shown in the great courts of the world, and every prince who saw it was overcome with admiration. One, in particular, fell head over heels in love with Faith.

The prince was named Warlock, for he'd won three great battles before he was eighteen. Warlock and his father were close friends. He went to his father, King Sage, and said, "I need your help. See, here's a portrait of Princess Faith. She has won my heart. Will you allow me to marry her?"

King Sage was delighted by Faith's happy, lovely face. "Such a pretty girl would gladden any court," he said. "I give you my blessing. I'll send Lord Converse as an ambassador to her father."

Young Converse was Warlock's best friend. He was a billionaire, and good at persuading people. He ordered a great retinue to accompany him. There were fifty diamonded gold carriages full of lords, and twenty-four hundred men on horseback.

When Converse said good-by, Warlock shook his hand warmly, saying, "If you're my friend, do what you can to win the princess. My life depends on marrying her. Give her these gifts for me."

He gave Converse a thousand fine gifts for Faith. One of them was his portrait.

Faith's parents were glad when they heard

that Converse was on his way. They approved of Warlock. They knew Warlock was the best, the bravest, the truest, and altogether the most suitable prince for their daughter.

The king thought that Converse should be presented to Faith. But Tulip Fairy said, "Majesty, it's not safe. Above all, don't let her go back to Warlock with him. Some dreadful thing might happen."

The queen agreed that Tulip Fairy spoke rightly.

The court enjoyed Converse's arrival. It took a whole day for his splendid retinue to enter the city. After the ceremonies and speeches of welcome, he asked to see the princess. To his surprise, he was refused.

The king said, "Please do not take offense. Let me tell you of my daughter's gifts from the fairies." Then he told Converse the whole story, ending with Well Fairy's threat.

"But Sire," Converse protested, "Warlock is deeply in love. He can't eat. He can't sleep. He sits sadly in corners. He is becoming very ill. Here, let me show you his portrait. Perhaps it will help you to decide."

He opened the portrait. The king and queen were pleased by Warlock's noble expression. Converse added his best arguments. "Forgive me, Sire, but it is beneath Your Majesty's dignity to care what mere fairies say. And if Warlock doesn't see Faith soon, he'll be too ill to marry anyone."

"Poor young prince," said the king. "He loves my daughter as she deserves. I was young once, myself. We'll see what we can do."

The king asked the queen to show Faith the portrait. Faith was very taken by it.

"Would you be wretched if you had a husband like that?" asked the queen, laughing.

Faith said, shyly, "It's not for me to choose a husband. I'll be glad to accept whomever you choose. I am sure that you know what is best."

"But if it were this one," teased the queen, "would you be pleased?"

Faith blushed, and looked away. Her mother kissed her. "Tomorrow we'll decide what to do," said the queen.

By then, Faith had grown to love Warlock from his portrait. Lady Weed, her lady-in-waiting, teased her about it, and so did Faith's maids of honor, who were Lady Weed's two daughters. One of them, Daisy, loved Faith loyally and well. The other, named Prickly, was jealous of Faith. She, too, had seen the portrait. She would have liked a rich, handsome prince like Warlock for her own husband.

Unfortunately, Prickly's godmother was the Well Fairy. That night, the jealous girl went to see the fairy, and said, "Faith is going to marry Warlock. But I want to marry him myself. Can't you help me?"

Well Fairy remembered Faith only too well. "That wretched girl again!" she cried. "It will be a pleasure to ruin her hopes." She whispered in Prickly's big ear, and a broad smile spread over the girl's face. As soon as she got home she told her mother, Lady Weed, about the Well Fairy's plot.

Now Faith had been thinking all night how she could cheer the sick Warlock by coming to him at once. She didn't want to wait three months until her fifteenth birthday. At last she sent for her mother.

"Can't we fool the Fairy?" asked Faith. "Send me to Warlock in a windowless, covered carriage. At night, a guard could open it and serve supper. That way I'd be safe. And I could cure the prince's misery, too."

The queen agreed to the idea, and so did the king. They told Converse that Faith would leave next day. Delighted, he made ready to leave, so that he could hurry home and tell

Warlock and his court to expect Faith. He did not even see the princess, but he sent her a message of thanks. He was anxious to relieve Warlock's mind.

The king had a closed carriage made. It was covered with green velvet outside. The inside was hung with rose brocade, embroidered in silver. The carriage shut up tighter than a box, allowing no daylight to enter. Only the highest lord in the land held the keys to its doors.

So that the travelers could move quickly only a few guards were sent to accompany them. Trunks full of fabulously lovely clothes and jewels were piled into the carriage. At last everything was ready, and Faith got in, followed by Lady Weed, Daisy, and Prickly.

The queen trusted Lady Weed. "Lady Weed," she said, "I count on you. My dearest treasure, Faith, is in your care. Watch out for her. Above all, don't let her see daylight. Warlock will have a palace ready. She won't see daylight from it. It's up to you to get her safely inside it."

The queen gave Lady Weed rich presents to show her gratitude for Lady Weed's protection of her daughter.

Lady Weed took the gifts, and said, "Don't worry. Leave it all to me."

They set out. Each evening of the journey the lords brought them their supper, and told them how much further they had to go to reach Warlock's court.

"Mother," Prickly whispered to Lady Weed, "you must do something, before it is too late. I shall die if I can't marry Warlock."

Next day, at high noon, Lady Weed took out a long knife that she had hidden. With it she slashed the carriage's velvet roof from front to back. Daylight poured in.

For the first time, Faith saw the sun. She gasped with shock, and then immediately turned into a white deer. Terrified, she leaped out and ran off into the forest.

The Well Fairy's plot was working well. The lords and guards rode off in all directions to look for the white deer. To stop them, Well Fairy stirred up a storm. Lightning came so thick that the guards and lords dared not move. Then the fairy transported them all, helpless, to a magic land.

Of Faith's companions only Lady Weed, Daisy, and Prickly were left. Daisy ran into the forest, calling her princess.

The other two continued to carry out the plot. Prickly put on Faith's wedding gown. She hid her bony shoulders under the glorious wedding cape, and stuck the diamond crown on her stubby hair. Then she seized a ruby scepter in her claw of a hand. She was ready now to meet Warlock and to make believe that she was Faith.

Prickly headed for Warlock's court, Lady Weed trotting behind and holding her train. They were sure that Warlock would be waiting nearby to meet his princess. And indeed, it was not long before they saw horsemen gathered around a gold open carriage. In the carriage sat the old king and his lovesick son, Warlock. Two lords galloped up to the finely dressed ladies, and dismounted.

Said Prickly, in a fancy voice, "Do tell me, who is in the gold carriage?"

"Our king, and his son, Prince Warlock. They're waiting for Princess Faith," said one of the lords.

"Do give them this message, then," twittered Prickly. "A jealous fairy stole my attendants with lightning and other magic. Only my lady-in-waiting remained with me. She has my jewels, and letters for the king."

The lords kissed the hem of her robe. Then they hurried back to tell the king and his son.

Warlock cried, "Isn't she glorious? Isn't she the loveliest girl alive? Isn't she?"

The lords did not answer. Surprised, Warlock said, "Has her beauty struck you dumb?"

"Majesty," said the bolder lord, "you'll see for yourself."

The king and his son, followed by the court, went to meet the ladies. When the king saw Prickly he cried, "Is this a joke?"

Lady Weed stepped forward. "Sire," she said, "here is the Princess Faith. And here are letters from her father, the king. In these boxes are her jewels."

The king was too busy staring to answer. Warlock, too, was gaping at the sight of the great galumphing girl. Her bony knees stuck out under the dress. Her parroty nose pointed down, her chin pointed up to meet it, and her crookedy teeth grinned.

Warlock with an effort made himself speak. "I've been cheated," he said. "The portrait I've loved is nothing like this individual. They have fooled us. This cruel trick will be the death of me."

"What's that?" cried Prickly. "Who has been fooled? I will make a perfect wife for you."

Lady Weed shrilled, "Is this how you foreign creatures treat a royal princess? My poor Princess Faith, your royal father would die if he knew."

"He'll know, never fear. He promised us the exquisite princess of the portrait. He's sent a horse's skeleton in her place. We won't be cheated so," said the king.

The king and Warlock got back into their carriage. Two guards slung Lady Weed and Prickly behind them on their horses. The king ordered them to be held prisoner in one of his castles.

Warlock was too upset to bear the gay life at court. He told Converse he wanted to retire from the world to a lonely spot, where quiet might heal his broken heart. As soon as he was well enough, he prepared to leave. He wrote his father a letter, saying he'd come back when he could be gay again, and asking that the ugly Faith and her lady be kept prisoner.

Then Warlock and Converse rode off together. At the end of three days, while they were still deep in a forest, the tired prince felt that he could go no further. He lay on the soft grass to rest, while Converse went to find them a place to pass the night.

Had the prince but known it, his beloved princess, in the shape of the magic white deer, was not very far away. She had been trying to get used to her new four-footed self. She had, at least, the joy of being a lovely, lively deer, just as she had been a lovely, lively princess.

She found she liked to eat grass. She liked to lie on mossy banks. But most of all she loved the sunlight she had never seen till now. The world shone gay and clear before her.

Tulip Fairy knew of Faith's mishap. She wasn't pleased at what had happened, for had she not warned Faith and her mother that the princess must not see daylight? Still, she loved Faith dearly, and she did what she could to help her. She led Daisy, who was searching through the forest, toward the princess. Daisy was astonished when a white deer come bounding up to her. She looked closer, and saw by the deer's eyes that the animal recognized her. Daisy knew it must be her princess.

Daisy curtsied. "Dearest princess," she said, "we'll stay together always. I'll do my best to serve you."

The white deer showed her joy by giving a graceful leap. Then she led Daisy, who was hungry, to some fruit trees. As Daisy ate, she wondered where she would spend the night.

"Aren't you afraid," she asked Faith, "when it's dark, and the wolves howl?"

The deer nodded.

"Have you seen any people or houses in this forest?" asked Daisy.

The deer shook her head.

"Whatever shall we do?" wondered Daisy.

Their problem touched Tulip Fairy's heart. She appeared, and said, "I will help you. I can't do much, but I can make the period of your enchantment easier to bear. Every night after sunset, Faith, you'll turn into yourself. You'll remain Princess Faith all night. But at dawn you must become a white deer once more. Well Fairy is very powerful."

The white deer leapt gracefully to show her thanks.

"Now, go this way," said Tulip Fairy. "There's a neat little cabin down this path. Be brave until we meet again." Then the good fairy vanished.

Daisy and the deer soon came to the cabin. An old woman sat sunning herself at the door. Daisy curtsied. "Do you have a room to give me and my deer?" she asked.

"Yes, I do, young lady," said the woman. She showed Daisy a pleasant room. It was white and neat and had twin beds. Many years later, Faith said it was the prettiest room she'd ever had.

At sundown, Faith became herself again. She hugged Daisy, and thanked her for her loyalty.

They talked for a long while before they went to bed. At dawn, Faith would be a deer again. She would run off into the forest to exercise her supple legs, as deer do.

Now Converse was still searching the forest for a place where he and Warlock could spend the night. Early that evening he came to the cabin and asked the old woman if she could

help him. Smiling, she gave him a big basket of apples and pears, and said, "Bring your friend back whenever you wish." She showed him a pleasant room that was right next to Daisy's room.

Converse brought Warlock to the cabin, and they both slept well after their long ride. The next morning Warlock rose early and went walking. He jumped with surprise as a splendid white deer flashed past him. He loved hunting. "What a good thing I brought my bow and arrows!" he thought, and started after the deer.

The deer ran her best, with Warlock following close. Now and then his arrows almost hit her, for he was a good shot. More than once Tulip Fairy had to turn aside his arrows, or he would have killed the deer.

The deer was all but exhausted as sunset drew near. She made a last, desperate turn, and Warlock lost her trail. The deer limped to the cabin, and stretched on the floor. Daisy stroked her shoulder, and wondered what had happened. At last the sun set, and the deer turned into Faith.

She told Daisy her day's adventures with the hunter. "He's more dangerous than Well Fairy," she said. "I didn't even see him. But he saw me only too well. He almost hit me, more than once."

"Dearest princess, stay inside. Don't leave this room until your enchantment is over," said Daisy. "I'll buy some books in the nearest town. I'll read to you all day long. We'll have fun. Don't go into danger again."

"I'd stay here if I could," said Faith. "But when I am a deer, I feel like a deer. I must run and leap and eat grass. I can't bear being indoors."

Faith was so tired that she fell asleep instantly. In the room next door Warlock was talking to Converse of his exciting deer hunt.

"I never saw a finer deer," he said. "She ran like the wind. Tomorrow I'll hunt her again."

Converse was glad to hear his prince talk of something besides his broken heart. He encouraged Warlock to sleep early, and be ready to hunt in the morning.

Next day, Warlock went where he'd seen the deer before. Faith was afraid of the spot now. She had gone to the quiet of the deep woods. Warlock walked and walked, deep into the forest, tracking the white deer. He grew hot and hungry, and when he came to an apple tree he ate some apples, and lay down to sleep. Soon the deer came by and saw the sleeping figure.

Faith realized it was her beloved Warlock. She knelt beside him. "He's much handsomer than his portrait," she thought. She lay down beside him, forgetting her own danger.

When Warlock woke, he stared in astonishment, for there beside him was the white deer. The deer leapt in terror and dashed into the woods, with Warlock following. The deer would rather have gone toward her beloved prince than away. But she had to run from him for her life.

Finally the white deer tired, and her steps grew slower. Warlock tried a shot. She sped on unhurt, light as the wind. But as she crossed an open glade, he aimed true. The arrow pierced her leg and she fell to the ground.

When Warlock saw the deer helpless, he was sorry he'd hurt her. He gathered herbs and bound up the wound.

It was late in the day when he carried her to the cabin. Daisy saw them coming, and ran out, horrified. "Beg pardon, sir," she said, "but that's my deer."

"It is my deer," said Warlock, as graciously as he could. "I caught her in the woods."

"I'd sooner lose my life than lose my deer," said Daisy. "See how she knows me."

She said, "White deer, shake hands." The deer gave her her right paw.

She said, "White deer, touch my left shoulder," and the deer touched her shoulder.

She said, "White deer, do you love me?" The deer nodded her head.

The prince was convinced. "I agree," he said, "she's yours. I'm sorry I hurt her. I'm sorry to have to give her up, too."

Daisy brought the deer into the cabin. She did not know that anyone else was staying there.

Warlock and Converse saw Daisy and the deer go ahead of them into the cabin. Converse wore a puzzled frown, for he, too, had thought they were the old woman's only guests. Converse asked the old woman where the young lady's room was.

"Right next to yours," she said. "There is only a wall between your two rooms."

Converse hurried with Warlock to their room. He said, "Highness, I'm sure that young woman is Princess Faith's maid of honor. I saw her at court."

"Then why is she here?" asked Warlock.

"I intend to find out," said Converse. He made a tiny hole in the wall.

Warlock paid no heed. He looked dreamily out the window, thinking of his lost Faith. Converse made the hole big enough to peep through. He looked, and saw Faith in a dazzling silver gown. Daisy was bending over her, bandaging her arm.

"Highness," said Converse, almost bursting with excitement, "come here, I beg you. Come and see the original of your beloved portrait."

The prince took one look at Faith and felt his heart flood with joy. He ran from the room and knocked at the princess' door. When Daisy opened it, Warlock rushed in and threw himself on his knees before Faith. "Forgive me," he cried. "How could I know? I'd sooner die than hurt you."

Faith assured him that her wound was slight and that, indeed, it had now brought her happiness.

All night the four of them talked of their marvelous adventures, and their hopes for a more marvelous future. Day broke without their noticing it. It was late morning when Faith suddenly realized she was still herself, though the sun rode high.

Now their joy knew no bounds. Faith need never run, four-footed, into the woods again.

"We must tell my father at once," Warlock said. "He is about to start a terrible war of revenge with your family, for he thinks that they tricked him."

Just then, a sound of trumpets rang through the woods. Warlock looked out. He recognized a troop of officers, and ordered them to halt. They were the vanguard of his father's army. The king himself was there, in a gold open carriage. Behind him, on a farm wagon, came Prickly and Lady Weed.

Warlock ran to his father. "Majesty, hear this," he cried. He explained everything. Then he asked Faith to come forth. She rode out on a prancing horse, looking as dazzling as a sky full of stars. She wore a silver hunting costume, studded with diamonds. A hundred plumes danced over her head. Daisy, who followed, was almost as lovely.

It was Tulip Fairy who had cured Faith's arm, and dressed them both in gorgeous clothes. The cabin in the woods had been her invention, too. The old woman was Tulip Fairy herself, in disguise.

The king was enchanted. "I beg you," he said to Faith, "give my kingdom the loveliest queen in the world. Marry this son of mine. I'll give him my throne, and you two will rule in my stead."

"Whatever you ask me to do, I'll do, Majesty," said Faith. "It is my pleasure as well as my duty." Then she spied Prickly and her mother. She never held grudges. She said, "Pardon them, my lord. Give them the wagon they ride in to take them wherever they wish. Please!"

The king granted her wish. Her forgiving nature pleased him.

In triumph, at the head of a great army, Warlock and Faith went back to his castle. Tremendous wedding preparations were made. On the day of the wedding the six flower fairies came, showering gifts and joy on all.

A final touch of joy came when Daisy agreed to marry Converse. Daisy knew his good heart, and his high rank in a country strange to her. Tulip Fairy gave Daisy a dowery of four gold mines in the Indies, so that she would be at least as rich as her husband.

The two couples were married on the same day, amid great rejoicing. The whole country delighted for years in telling and retelling the story of the marvelous white deer.

Beauty and the Beast

Once there was a very rich trader who had three sons and three daughters. All the girls were beautiful, but the loveliest one of all was the youngest. She was named Beauty, and this made her sisters very jealous. They hated her kind ways and fair face. They only liked rich, silly people and parties. They laughed at Beauty, who liked to read, and help at home.

Suddenly misfortune came to the trader and he lost all his money in business. He had nothing left but a small farm. "We'll have to live in the country," he said, "and work the farm. If we're good farmers, we'll have plenty to eat, at least."

On the farm, the man and his sons worked in the fields. Beauty got up each day at dawn. She cleaned the house, and got breakfast ready. It was hard at first, for she was not used to work. But soon she became capable and strong.

Her sisters sat around all day moping, and doing nothing. Just to see Beauty work made them cross.

When they had lived for a year on the farm, good news came for the trader. One of his ships, laden with cargo, had come safely to port. He made ready to go to the city to see about it. The older girls hoped to be rich again, and they asked their father to bring them lots of new clothes.

"What would you like?" the trader asked Beauty.

"Perhaps you'll bring me a rose," said Beauty. "I can't seem to grow them here."

In town, the father used most of the money from the ship's goods to pay old debts. He started home as poor as when he'd left. Halfway home, he rode into a deep forest, and lost his way. It began to snow thick and fast. The wind raged. Night had fallen and the wolves were howling all around. The merchant didn't know where to turn.

Suddenly he saw lights shining among the trees. A castle, brightly lit, lay inside a wide park. Thankfully, the trader hurried to the gate. The courtyard was empty. He stabled his horse, and went in the open door of the castle. Inside, he saw a friendly fire. A table was set for one, with good food in plenty.

He went to the fire, thinking, "The owner will surely pardon me for taking refuge here. I hope he comes in soon."

He waited for hours. No one came. He was so hungry that at last he sat down and ate. Then he walked through the other rooms. They were all beautiful and well kept, but he saw no one. When he came to a bedroom he was so tired he went to bed.

He woke late next morning. He blinked in surprise, for a fine new suit lay in place of the damp, old one he'd worn the day before.

"A kind fairy must own this castle," he thought. He looked out the window. The snow was gone, and masses of flowers brightened in the sun. He turned back to his room, and saw a tray laden with buttered rolls and a pot of chocolate.

"Kind fairy," he said aloud, "you're most thoughtful. Thank you." He had a good breakfast.

Outside, he found his horse already saddled, and he set out for home. As he rode under a trellis heavy with roses he thought of Beauty's wish, and picked a rose for her.

Just then there was a terrible roar, and a monstrous beast rushed up. "I saved your life, and you show your thanks by stealing my precious roses. You'll die for this. Say your prayers, for in ten minutes I'll kill you."

"Majesty, forgive me," begged the trader. "I took the rose for one of my daughters. She asked me to bring her one."

"My name is not Majesty," roared the creature. "My name is Beast. I hate flattery. You say you have daughters. Go home to them. Ask if one of them will die instead of you. If they refuse, you must return yourself in three months."

The trader had no idea of letting his girls die for him. He thought, "I'll go, and say farewell to my family." He swore to return in three months.

Beast said, "You may leave now. I'll send you a trunk full of gold when you get home."

"What a strange beast," thought the trader. "He's cruel and kind at the same time." He left the castle. His horse seemed to know the right road of his own accord, and soon the trader was home. The sight of his children waiting for him made him weep.

He gave Beauty the rose, saying, "I paid a high price for this."

Then he told his story.

The older girls howled and scolded Beauty. "Why couldn't you be satisfied with new clothes, like us? You had to be special. You've cost us our father's life. And you don't even cry for it!"

"Why cry?" said Beauty quietly. "Father won't die. Beast said I might take his place. And I shall, gladly."

"No," said her brothers. "We'll go after this monster. If we can't kill him, we'll die fighting."

"Beast has magic powers we can't fight," said the father. "Beauty means well. But I shan't let her go. I'm old. I'll soon die, anyway. I only regret leaving you all, my dears."

But Beauty stood firm. "Father, I must go," she said. "I'd sooner let Beast kill me than die of grief over causing your death."

Finally, Beauty had her way. Her sisters were secretly glad to be rid of her.

When the trader went to his room, he found a trunk full of gold on his bed. Beast hadn't forgotten. He called Beauty, and showed her the gold.

"Good," she said. "Two gentlemen want to marry my sisters. This gold can be their wedding present." Her kind heart never held grudges.

Beauty and her father left the next day. Her brothers wept. Her sisters rubbed their eyes with onions, and wept, too.

The horse found the way to the castle by himself, and the trader led Beauty in. There was a table set for two with gold plates and crystal glasses and fine food. They sat down to dinner.

Beauty tried to be calm. She thought, "Beast wants me to fatten up, so I'll taste good when he eats me."

After dinner, Beast came in with a loud roar. Beauty was afraid, but she tried to hide her fears.

"Did you come here willingly?" asked Beast.

"Yes," Beauty said, in a small voice.

"You are good. I'm grateful to you," said Beast. "Sir," he said to her father, "leave here tomorrow. Don't come back. Now, good night, Beauty."

"Good night, Beast," she said.

Beast left, and Beauty and her father went to their rooms to sleep. While she slept, Beauty dreamed of a lady who said, "Beauty, your good heart will bring you great rewards." Next day, she told her father her dream. It made him feel better. Even so, he was sad as he left her.

Beauty thought bravely, "I can do nothing to help myself now. So I shan't worry. I'll be happy while I can. Beast probably won't eat me until tonight, so I have all day to explore."

She wandered over the castle. Each room was more lovely than the next. At last she came to a paneled door, on which was a sign that said, "Beauty's Apartment." Shyly, she opened the door. She saw the room of her dreams. It was lined with shelves of books. There was a grand piano, and many books of music.

"Why does Beast take such pains to please me, if he's going to eat me tonight?" she wondered.

On the table was a golden placard that said, "Beauty rules here. Beauty's wish is our command."

"My wish," sighed Beauty, "is to know what father is doing now." She glanced up. A mirror on the wall shone with a clear reflection of the inside of her home. Her father looked very sad. The image left the mirror as fast as it had come.

"How kind Beast is," thought Beauty. "I'm not so afraid of him now."

That night, as she sat at supper, she heard Beast coming.

"Beauty," he said, "may I watch you have supper?"

"You're the master here," she answered.

"No," said Beast. "In this house, your wish is law. Tell me, do you find me very ugly?"

"Yes," said Beauty. "I can't lie. But I believe you are also very good."

"Yes," said Beast. "But I'm still an ugly, stupid Beast."

"Not stupid," smiled Beauty. "Stupid folk don't know they're stupid."

"Eat your supper," said Beast. "This castle is yours. Try to be happy in it."

"Your kindness makes me forget you're ugly," said Beauty. "Many men are more truly beasts than you. A good heart and an ugly face are better than a fair face and a rotten heart."

"I'm too stupid to thank you nicely," Beast growled. "But I am grateful for your good opinion."

Beauty had almost forgotten to be afraid of the monster, when he said, "Beauty, will you marry me?"

Beauty was silent. At last she said, honestly and simply, "No, Beast."

Beast gave a mighty sigh. "Good night, Beauty," he said, and left.

Three quiet months passed. Each night, Beast came while Beauty had supper. Each day, he proved his kindness. Beauty lacked for nothing. The only sad moment came at night, when Beast said, "Will you marry me?" and Beauty refused.

One night, she added, "You'll always be dear

to me, Beast. I'm truly your friend. But I don't think I shall ever be able to marry you."

"You're my only joy," said Beast. "I'd die without you. Promise, at least, that you'll never leave."

Beauty blushed, for that day her mirror had shown her her father, lying ill. She had been longing to go and comfort him.

"I promise never to leave you for good," she said. "But I long to see my father. I'll die if I can't go to him."

"I can't let you suffer," said Beast. "You may go home. You'll stay there, and I'll die of grief."

"No," said Beauty. "We're friends. I promise I'll be back. The mirror tells me that my sisters are married. My brothers are in the army. Father's alone. Give me a week with him."

"You'll wake at home tomorrow," said Beast. "When you want to come back here, just put your ring on the table as you go to bed. Good night, Beauty." And Beast sighed an even mightier sigh than usual.

Beauty awoke next day in her own home. A gold and diamond gown lay ready to wear. She put it on, inwardly thanking Beast for his kindness, and went downstairs.

Her father hugged her, and laughed, and cried for joy, all at the same time. Servants were sent to tell her sisters that Beauty had returned. They came, hoping for the worst. They were sorely disappointed. Beauty, dressed like a queen, was lovely as the daystar.

The two jealous sisters went off, gossiping. "Did you see that little snip in her gold gown? We'll have to spoil her game," whined one.

"Suppose we keep her here more than a week? She'd break her promise to Beast. Then maybe he'd eat her, at last," said the other.

"What a good idea!" said the first one. "We'll have to be very sweet to her."

The sisters were so sweet and loving to her

that Beauty cried for joy. When the week was up, the sisters stormed and wept. They made such a show of sadness that Beauty said she'd stay another week.

On the tenth night, Beauty dreamed. She thought she saw Beast lying on the grass, dying of despair. She woke up, regretting her cruelty. "He can't help being ugly," she thought. "He's good, and that is worth more than anything. I'm sorry I've hurt him."

She put her ring on the table, and went to sleep. Next morning, she was in Beast's castle again. She put on his favorite dress to please him, and waited impatiently for the evening. At last it was suppertime, time for Beast to appear.

But he did not come.

"What if I've killed him?" thought Beauty. She looked everywhere for Beast. Then she ran into the garden, remembering her dream. There lay Beast, quite still. Beauty bent over him, quite forgetting his ugliness. His heart still beat faintly. She ran for water, and dashed it on him.

Beast opened his eyes. He whispered, "I couldn't live without you. I'll die happy, now that you're here."

"No, Beast. You mustn't die. Live, and let me be your wife. I thought we were only friends. But I couldn't bear to lose you. I love you, Beast."

At Beauty's word, the castle sprang into light. Fireworks and music filled the air. Beast disappeared, and in his place stood a handsome prince.

"But where is Beast?" cried Beauty.

"I am he," said the prince. "I was enchanted by a powerful witch and became a monstrous beast. I had to stay that way until a beautiful girl should love me, and love me for my goodness alone. In all the world only you could help me, for only you are so good that goodness is enough to win your love. I beg you to be my queen."

Beauty gave the prince her hand, and he led her into the castle. There, to Beauty's joy, she found all her family. The lady Beauty had dreamed of, her first night in the castle, had brought them there.

"Beauty," said the lady, who was an important fairy, "come into the rewards of your virtue. You preferred goodness to looks and wit. So, you will find looks, wit, and goodness, all in one person who loves you. You are to be a great queen."

Then she turned to Beauty's sisters. "As for you, you'll be stone statues at the door of your sister's palace. Your only punishment will be to see your sister's happiness. Your enchantment will end the day you realize your wickedness and grow kind. But I fear that day may never come."

The fairy waved her wand. They were all transported to the prince's true kingdom, where his people acclaimed him with joy.

He and Beauty were married. They lived long and happily. Their joy was great, for it grew out of great goodness.

Silvershod

Once upon a time there was an old man named Vania. He was all alone in the world, and one day he decided to adopt a child, for company.

But what child would like him well enough to come and live with him, Vania wondered. Children can't belong to just anybody, as if they were kittens.

When his neighbor heard of Vania's plan, he said, "I know the very child. When Gregory Kara and his wife died, they left three children. The older girls have gone away to work as cooks. Dara, the third girl, is only six. She's still in her parents' home. A big family lives there now, and they don't want her."

"I thought I'd adopt a boy," said Vania.

"He'd learn to hunt, like me. I don't know much about girls."

Vania went home and thought. He remembered the Karas. They were gay, happy folk.

"If Dara's like them," he thought. "I'd never be sad again."

On Sunday, Vania dressed in his best and went to the next village, to the Kara's cabin. It was full of people of all sizes. In a corner sat a small, shy girl. A small, shy cat sat on her knees, purring.

Vania said to the mother of the big family, "Is that Dara Kara?"

"Yes," said the mother, crossly. "We have to feed and care for her, and that cat of hers besides. She's a nuisance."

102

Vania went to the little girl. "Will you come live with me, Dara?" he asked.

"How do you know my name?" asked Dara.

"I just know it," said Vania.

"Who are you?" asked Dara.

"I'm a hunter. Winters I hunt the stag no one ever sees. Summers I hunt for gold in the river."

"Do you want to kill the stag no one ever sees?" asked Dara.

"No, no," said Vania. "I kill the ordinary kind, for food. But this stag is different. I just want to see his silver hoof."

"Why?" asked Dara.

"That's a long story," said Vania. "If you come with me, you'll hear it."

Vania had kind eyes and a long white beard. Dara liked him. "I'll come," she said, "if I may bring Moura. She's my cat."

"Of course," said Vania. "Glad to have her. Her purr is better than a dozen violins."

The cross mother had already packed Dara's clothes, for she was afraid the old man might change his mind.

They walked to Vania's house. The old man walked tall and straight, his white beard flying. Dara skipped in circles around him. The cat trotted after, her tail in the air.

Vania, Dara, and Moura the cat made a happy family. Each one had a job. Vania hunted. Dara cleaned the house and got supper ready. Moura chased mice. They liked their jobs. In the evening, when they sat at the table, Vania said, "I'm glad we're together."

"Together, we're safe," said Dara.

"R-r-right you ar-r-re," purred Moura.

The hunter wasn't lonely any more. Dara wasn't frightened any more. Moura wasn't skinny any more.

Vania told lots of good stories. Once in a while Dara said, "Please, tell me about the stag with the silver hoof. You said you would."

And at last one day Vania began, "He's a remarkable stag. His right forefoot has a silver hoof. When he paws the ground with that hoof, jewels spark out from it." Then he said no more.

Soon he was sorry he'd said anything at all, for Dara never stopped asking about Silvershod.

"Is he bigger than ordinary stags?" she wanted to know.

"No, he's smaller," said Vania. "He stands no taller than you, on strong, slender legs."

"Has he horns?" asked Dara.

"He has," said Vania. "He has perfect, five-pointed antlers."

"Does he eat little girls?" asked Dara

"Deer never eat people. Silvershod crops grass and leaves," said Vania.

"What color is he?" Dara asked.

"He's red-brown in summer, the same color as Moura. In winter he's gray," answered Vania.

Autumn brought the hunting season. Vania left at dawn and came home at dark. He was looking for the herd of deer.

Dara wanted to go with him. "I might see Silvershod," she said.

"No," said Vania, kindly. "You can't tell Silvershod from the other stags in autumn. Now they all have five-pointed antlers. But in winter the others lose their antlers, and only Silvershod keeps his."

Next time, Vania was away five days. When he came back he said, "I've found the deer. They're beyond the forest. It's a big herd. I'll spend the winter there."

"How can you live in the forest in winter?" worried Dara.

"I have a hut there," said Vania. "It has a window, and a sturdy stove. It keeps me safe and warm, never fear."

"Is Silvershod there?" asked Dara.

"Who can tell?" smiled Vania.

"Take me with you," cried Dara. "I'll clean the hut for you, and cook. Silvershod might come by. I'd see him."

Vania shook his head. "No girl your age ever went to the forest in winter. It's lonely and dangerous. If you froze to death what would become of me?"

Dara kept asking to go, and at last Vania gave in.

"You may come," he said, "but don't complain if you find it hard, my dear."

Dara was delighted.

Vania got ready for the forest. He filled his sled with the supplies they would need for the winter. Dara got ready, too. She packed scraps of cloth to make doll's dresses, and she also packed a long cord.

"Perhaps Silvershod will let us catch him," she explained. "Then we'd need a cord, to lead him home."

Dara was sorry to leave Moura behind. She said, "You know, Moura, I almost got left behind, too. How would you live, out in the deep, snowy forest? You mind our hut here, while we're gone. As soon as I see Silvershod, I'll come back. I'll tell you all about it."

Moura smiled, and purred, "R-r-right you ar-r-re."

As Vania and Dara set off for the forest, the neighbors stared and whispered.

"Vania's crazy, to take a child into the forest," they said.

They left the village, and a red-brown streak shot past them. It was Moura. She kept just ahead of them, and out of sight, until it was too late to send her back. When they got to the hut in the forest, she appeared beside them.

Dara said to Vania, "It's more fun, when we're together, all three."

"Right you are," laughed Vania.

They went into the hut, and Moura at once curled up by the stove, and began to purr. "R-r-right you ar-r-re," she seemed to say.

That winter there were plenty of deer. Each day Vania caught one or two. Soon he had so many deerskin and so much meat that there was no room left to store them.

Dara knew Vania was wondering what to do. She said, "Vania, shouldn't you take the meat to the village, and bring back a big sled and a horse?"

"You're a thoughtful girl," said Vania. "Aren't you afraid to be left alone here?"

"No," said Dara. "It's a strong, cozy hut, and Moura will keep me company."

Vania went back to the village. The first days passed as usual, just as if Vania had gone hunting. At sunset, Dara watched Moura sleeping cozily by the stove. It kept her from feeling lonely.

She went to sit at the window. Sunset rays flashed down the snowy slopes. As Dara looked, a quick shape darted from a clump of trees. It was a small stag, with splendid five-pointed antlers.

Dara's heart pounded. She ran to the door, but when she looked out, nothing was there. "I must have been dreaming," she said.

The next day passed quietly. When evening came, Dara missed Vania. To cheer herself, she stroked Moura, and said, "Don't be sad, Moura, dear. Vania will be here tomorrow." The cat purred, and seemed to say, "R-r-right you ar-r-re."

Dara sat by the window, star-gazing. Suddenly she heard a clatter of hooves. She tried to hear where the noise came from. It went up over the roof-top, and down, right to the door-sill.

Dara tiptoed to the door, and opened it.

There was a small stag, with beautiful five-pointed antlers. He lifted his right forefoot, and Dara saw that it was solid silver.

She was so excited, she didn't know what to say. She clapped her hands. The stag laughed, and ran off.

Dara was sorry he'd left, but at least she had seen him. She hurried in to tell Moura. "If he comes again," she said, "maybe he'll strike the ground with his hoof, and make jewels fly out. How glad Vania would be!"

Moura purred, "R-r-right you ar-r-re."

The next day was quiet, like the others. Dara expected Vania that evening. He didn't come. She felt lonely, for Moura wasn't in her usual place by the stove.

She looked and looked, but she couldn't find Moura. Dara was worried. She went outside to search for the cat. It was late. A full moon blazed silver on the snow.

There, on a little hillock of snow, was Moura. Before her stood Silvershod. His right forefoot glinted in the moonlight. They seemed to be nodding their heads and talking together.

Moura ran off a little way. Silvershod followed. When he was close, he turned and dashed away, and Moura followed him. Further and further they went, in a game like a wild dance. Dara watched until they disappeared.

She waited to see if they'd return. They did. Silvershod came racing over the snow, Moura at his side.

He leapt atop the hut, and struck with his silver forefoot. As he struck, blue sparks leapt into the air. They fell to earth as bright sapphires. He struck and struck. Red sparks flew, and became rubies. Green sparks became emeralds. White sparks became diamonds.

Heaps and heaps and heaps of jewels tumbled, sparkling, from the roof.

Just then, Vania came. He could hardly see his hut under the rain and sparkle of precious stones. It was all a blaze of color and a flowering of light.

Up on the roof, Silvershod struck and struck with his hoof.

Suddenly Moura leapt up beside him with a strange cry that split the night. In an instant, Moura and Silvershod ran off and disappeared.

Silence fell. Vania pulled off his hat and filled it with jewels.

"Let's leave them here for tonight," said Dara. "Just think how they'll sparkle when the sun shines on them!"

Vania smiled and nodded. He took his hatful of jewels, and they went into the hut. It began to snow. Soon the jewels were hidden by a soft blanket of snow.

Next day Vania went to dig the jewels from under the snow. He dug and dug. But the jewels had completely disappeared.

He went inside, and counted the heap of jewels he'd put in his hat. He had plenty. They were worth enough to make any man comfortable for the rest of his days.

Old Vania and young Dara looked at each other, and smiled. They were happy. But they missed Moura. They never forgot her.

The strange thing is, neither Moura nor Silvershod was ever seen again.

Queen Cat

ONCE there was a king who had three fine sons. He feared one of them might want to be king in his place. Now although he was old, he didn't want to give up his throne yet, for he was still lively, and experienced in kingship. He decided to trick his sons into letting him rule in peace. He would keep them too busy to think of revolt.

He summoned them, and said, "You'll agree, I'm sure, I'm too old to be king much longer. One of you must take my place. I will give my crown to the one who finds me the best companion for my old age. I want a clever, faithful little dog. To the one who brings me the best, smallest dog I will give my crown."

The princes were surprised, but too respectful to disagree. Their father gave them each plenty of gold, and said, "I'll see you in exactly one year, with your dogs."

The three brothers swore to be friends, no matter who won. Then they went their own ways. They all had many fine adventures. But it's the youngest I shall tell you about now.

He was handsome, intelligent, and of a happy disposition. All the things a prince should do, he did well. He was learned, talented, and braver than a zooful of lions.

One evening, as the young prince was journeying through a forest, a storm broke. He had no idea where he was, and when he saw a light ahead, he made for it. He came to a magnificent castle. Its door was set with glittering jewels, and the walls were of crystal. They were etched with scenes from every fairy story: Cinderella, Thumbkin, Sleeping Beauty, and many more.

The doorknocker was a huge diamond. The prince knocked, and the door opened. He saw a dozen pairs of hands holding torches; but there were no bodies attached to the hands. The astonished prince didn't know whether to walk in or run away. As he hesitated, he felt other hands draw him inside. He walked warily, his hand on the hilt of his sword.

Hands led him to a coral door that opened as he neared it. He went through sixty rooms, and each room was hung with a fairyland of pictures. Lights from a thousand jeweled chandeliers blazed. The hands drew him to a halt in the sixty-first room. All by itself an easy chair moved close to the fire for him. Hands took off his wet things and put on fine dry ones, far richer than his own.

Then the hands led him to another room. Here the walls were painted with pictures of famous cats: Puss in Boots was there, and the Three Little Kittens who lost their mittens, and the Pussy Cat that went to London to look at the queen—and many more.

A table was set for two, with jeweled dishes. A beautiful snow-white cat came in, followed by a retinue of cats. "King's son, welcome," said the white cat. "We are pleased to see you."

"Most excellent Majesty," said the prince, "thank you for your royal aid. Indeed, you're a remarkable cat. I'm amazed by your delightful speech, and by your castle, which is marvelous beyond words."

"King's son," said Queen Cat, "you needn't flatter me. I like simple words and deeds. Won't you have dinner now?"

Hands served dinner—a mouse pie for Queen Cat, and a chicken pie for the prince. The sight of the queen's dish kept the prince from eating his. Queen Cat, guessing his thoughts, said, "Don't worry, king's son! Cats are cats, men are men, and my cooks are careful. You won't find mice in your pie."

The prince smiled, and ate well.

After supper, they went to the next room. There graceful cats in ballet costumes did Spanish and Chinese dances. Later, hands led the prince to bed in a charming room. Its walls were covered with flower pictures, made of shimmering butterfly wings and bird feathers.

Early next morning the prince was wakened by merry noises outside. He looked out of the window and saw the cat court was mounting for the hunt. Hands helped the prince to dress in hunting costume. He went down, and was given a gay wooden horse. To his delight, the horse trotted and galloped and cantered beautifully. It took fences like a dream. Queen Cat rode a monkey.

They hunted hare. When they had caught enough, Queen Cat led them home to a festive dinner. Afterwards, the prince drank a glass of golden liqueur. He soon forgot why he had left home. His search for a dog was forgotten. It was enough for him to stay in the castle and enjoy the clever, charming company of Queen Cat.

They often rode through the forest, and picnicked by a waterfall. They fished and hunted, read and wrote. They listened to music, or watched the cat ballet. They were served perfectly by hands that never tired.

Luckily, Queen Cat remembered what the prince had forgotten. One day she said, "Do you know, in three days you must give your father the dog he wants?"

"What on earth made me forget it?" cried the prince. "My life is ruined if I fail. But how can I find a dog, buy a horse, and get home, all in three days?"

Queen Cat smiled serenely. "King's son, be calm. I'm your friend. You may stay here one day more. The wooden horse will take you the five hundred miles to your home. He'll do it in twelve hours."

"I'm grateful," said the prince, "but what about the dog?"

"Here he is," said Queen Cat. She handed him an acorn.

The prince took it, wondering.

"Put it to your ear," she said.

He did. Inside the acorn shell sounded a clear, strong little bark.

"Keep it shut until you give it to your father," said the cat.

The prince was glad to have no more problems. "But," he said, "I'm sorry to leave you, Queen Cat. I owe you everything."

The prince got home ahead of his brothers. When his brothers came, they didn't know what to think of the wooden horse, prancing nobly in the courtyard. Then they wondered why the youngest prince seemed to have no dog. Of course, they could not see the tiny acorn.

The king sent for his sons. He admired the two elder brothers' lapdogs. Then the youngest took the acorn out of his pocket.

"Father," he said, "this is for you."

The king opened the acorn. From a velvet pillow leapt a perfect, tiny dog. The dog did a Spanish dance, lightly as a snowflake—and indeed, the dog was not much bigger than one.

However, the king was dismayed, for his trick had failed. His son had been too successful. The king still wanted to keep his crown, so he said, "My sons, thank you for the dogs. Now, prove your cleverness once again. Bring me a yard of cloth that will pass through the eye of this needle." He held up the finest, thinnest embroidery needle made. "Take a year to find the cloth," he said.

The princes weren't very pleased, but they set off obediently to find the cloth. The youngest son went straightway to Queen Cat. Her palace doors were flung wide in welcome. Fireworks blazed in celebration. Hands helped him from his wooden horse.

He and Queen Cat were glad to see each other. The prince told her how great a success the dog had been. Then he told her his father's new orders. She said, "Don't worry about it. The world's finest weavers are in my kingdom. In fact, I weave well myself. Work will begin at once on your yard of cloth."

The second year vanished like the first, in merriment and outings of all kinds.

The prince had all but forgotten home. Luckily, Queen Cat kept an eye on the calendar, and one day she said, "You must leave tomorrow to bring your father the cloth. A carriage and guards are ready to take you."

There was a rose-gold carriage drawn by twelve bold horses, followed by a hundred smaller carriages full of generals. There were a thousand bodyguards, in uniforms embroidered so thickly in gold you couldn't see the cloth beneath.

"Now you can go home in style," said Queen Cat. "Here's a walnut for your father. Open it before his eyes. The yard of cloth is inside."

"Dearest Queen Cat, you've been so good to me. I'd sooner let my father keep his crown than leave you," said the prince.

Queen Cat smiled. "You must do your duty," she said. "I'm grateful for your friendship. After all, I'm just a four-footed mouse trap."

The magnificent party of men traveled fast, and reached the king's palace in no time. The elder sons had already arrived. They presented their yards of cloth. The cloth was, in fact, very fine. It could pass through the eye of a shoemaker's needle. With a sly look, the king held up the embroidery needle they'd seen the year before. The cloth didn't even begin to go through. Their father was secretly glad they'd failed.

Then, amid trumpet fanfares, the youngest son arrived in all his magnificence. He greeted his family. Then he took out his walnut and split it. There was a pecan shell inside. He broke the pecan, and saw a cherry stone. Everyone began to whisper and smile. Inside the cherry stone was a kernel. At that the court laughed.

"Someone's made a fool of the youngest prince," they murmured.

The prince opened the kernel. Inside was a grain of wheat; inside that was a grain of rye. The prince began to be anxious. He opened the rye-grain.

He was almost as amazed as the king and all his courtiers, as he drew from inside the grain of rye six yards of wondrously fine cloth. Pictures were woven into it. It showed all the fish, birds, animals, trees, flowers, and plants on earth and under the sea. It showed the moon, the sun, the stars, the planets in their orbits. It showed all the rulers of the earth then alive, with their wives, their children, and their chief citizens. It passed, all six yards of it, six times through the eye of the needle with no trouble at all.

The king was none too pleased. But he had to exclaim at the beauty of the wonderful length of cloth. Hiding his sighs, and trying to show joy, he said, "It pleases me to see how devoted you are to an old man's wishes. I don't want to deprive you of the chance to obey me once more before I give up my crown. This time, go and bring back a beautiful girl to be your bride. Whoever finds the loveliest girl will win my crown on his wedding day."

The princes were too well brought up to contradict their father. They left for the third time. The youngest went, with all his company, back to Queen Cat.

"Well, king's son," said the white cat, "here you are again, and still uncrowned."

"It's not your fault I didn't win the crown," said the prince. "I suspect my father really wants to keep his crown for himself."

"No matter," said the queen, "it's your duty to do all you can to be worthy of the crown, whether you get it or not. I understand that this time you must find a beautiful girl who is willing to marry you. I'll find you one."

The third year went as quickly as the first two. The prince and Queen Cat played chess, hunted, fished, and read aloud.

Soon it was time for the prince to return home. The day before he had to leave Queen Cat said, "Now, this time it's up to you. You may, if you wish, bring back one of the fairest

and richest princesses in the world. Change me back to my human self, and you'll see."

"Good!" cried the prince. "How can I make you human, dearest Queen Cat?"

"Cut off my head and my tail," said the queen. "Throw them onto the fire."

"Cut off your head and tail?" cried the prince. "You're dearer to me than a dozen kingdoms. I won't hurt a hair of your head."

"You must," she said gently. "It can be the beginning of great joy for us both."

He still hesitated. She insisted. At last she convinced him, and he drew his sword. His hand shook with horror. But he cut off the head and tail, and threw them on the fire.

And the marvel happened. Before him stood an exquisite girl, gracious enough to win every heart, and lovely enough to keep every eye entranced forever.

Hundreds of noble lords and ladies filed into the room. Each had a cat-skin over his shoulder. They bowed before the fair young queen, and vowed homage to her. She spoke a while with them. Then she asked to be left alone with the prince.

"I want to tell you my story," she said.

This is the story she told. I know you want to hear it too.

"I have not always been a cat," she said. "My father was king of six kingdoms, and my mother loved to travel in them. On one of her travels she heard of a fairy castle in whose garden was grown the best fruit in the world. Mother wanted some of this fruit. She went to the castle gate, but no one answered her summons. There was no way to get inside the high golden walls.

"She couldn't eat or sleep, for wanting that fruit. One night as she lay abed, sick with longing, an old woman came and sat beside her.

" 'Queen,' said the old woman, 'you are a

Adrienne Ségur

nuisance, with your wishes for fruit. But you seem to be dying without it. So my sisters and I have decided to ignore your bad manners, and give you some fruit. But we want something in exchange.'

"'Good woman, tell me quickly what you want,' said the queen. 'I'd give anything for that fruit of yours.'

"'You must give us the daughter you'll soon have. We'll give her beauty, and goodness. We'll bring her up wisely and well. But you may not see her until she is twenty.'

"'You drive a hard bargain,' said the queen. 'But I accept.'

"The queen called in her maids, dressed, and followed the fairy woman into the castle garden. Then the fairy called out, 'Apricots, peaches, plums, pears, cherries, blueberries, huckleberries, strawberries, raspberries, blackberries, oranges, lemons, grapes, melons, apples of every kind, come ye here to me.'

"Fruit came floating through the air and piled itself up gently in great heaps. My mother ate as much as she could. Then the fairies filled a thousand baskets with their fruit that could not spoil. They loaded the baskets onto the backs of five hundred donkeys. My mother took the fruit home. She had enough for months of court dinners.

"Soon after, I was born. My mother hated to think of her strange bargain. She was ashamed to tell my father, and fell into deep misery. My father was worried, and at last she had to tell him. He was furious. He locked her in a tower, and got a nurse to care for me.

"But fairies always play fair. Cheating makes them rage. They sent curse after curse over my father's kingdoms. My father went to an old fairy friend of his, and asked what he should do.

"'I can't help,' she answered. 'You've wronged my sisters. You'd best keep your wife's bargain. Give the princess to the fairies and let your wife out of her prison. She's a fine woman, who meant no harm. Keep her word as if it were your own. You'll be glad if you do, I promise.'

"My father obeyed. He and my mother put me in a jeweled crib and brought me to the fairies. They received me with great joy, and took me to a tower that they built especially for me. It had a thousand different rooms, for every season and occasion you can imagine, and on the roof was a pleasant garden. There were no doors to the tower, only high windows. The fairies taught me everything under the sun, and lessons were better than games, when the fairies taught them.

"I'd have been glad to stay there all my life, if they hadn't decided it was time for me to marry. They chose the fairy King Tiny as my husband. Parrot, an old friend, came to talk over the news.

"'Poor lovely princess,' he said, 'I'm so sorry for you.'

"'Why?' I asked.

"'King Tiny is why,' said Parrot. 'He's a frightening, ugly fellow. He gives me the creeps. He's mean. I know him well. He was brought up in the same tree I lived in.'

"'In the same tree?' I exclaimed.

"'Yes,' said Parrot. 'He has eagles' claws for feet.'

"Just then Fairy Fierce came in, and said, 'Hurry and dress.' She gave me the prettiest dress of all my pretty dresses. 'King Tiny's here,' she said. 'Make yourself pretty for him. Here are some diamonds to match the dress.'

"'But I haven't said I want to marry him, or even see him,' I cried.

"'Silly child, how dare you speak to me that way?'

"I went on, 'I'm miserable here, anyway,

cooped up all the time with a parrot and a lot of old women.'

"Fairy Fierce raged. 'I've always known you'd be an ungrateful wretch,' she said. 'Wait till my sisters hear this.'

"I didn't dress up for King Tiny. I put up my hair crooked, on purpose. Then I went out on the terrace to meet him. He shuffled up to me on eagle claws, half on his knees. He was a tiny, cranky dwarf. His head was the size of an orange. His nose was sharp and long as a pencil. He wanted to kiss my cheek in greeting, and asked his servant to lift him up to reach it. But he never did. I locked myself in my room.

"King Tiny went home, insulted. The fairies were cross with me. Fairy Fierce convinced them I was hopelessly wicked.

"They brought me back to one of my father's palaces, the one where we are now. They changed me, and all the lords and ladies of the kingdom, into cats. One of the kinder fairies whispered that some day a prince would rescue me. That prince is you. You've ended all my troubles."

"Will you end my troubles, too?" asked the youngest prince. "Will you marry me?"

"I love you better than life," said the queen. "Now we must go to your father. Let's see what he thinks of me."

They went to the prince's home together, in a splendid carriage. The trip seemed even shorter than the others, for the queen and the prince had many delightful plans to make.

As they neared the palace, the queen hid in a hollow rock crystal. It was like a star, with rubies at the points. A heavy curtain covered it. Six strong soldiers carried it ahead of the prince's carriage.

The elder brothers were walking in the courtyard with their lovely princesses. They came to meet him, asking where his lady was.

"I saw only ugly princesses," he said. "Instead, I've brought a rare white cat."

"A cat? I wonder what father will say to that," they said, laughing.

"We'll see," said the youngest.

They went to the throne room. The two princesses were presented to the king. A lovely sight they were, both fair and modest.

Then came the youngest son. The rock crystal was carried in after him, and set down before the throne. The prince drew the curtain. "Aaa-aaah!" gasped the court, at the beauty of the great starry jewel.

"Inside this crystal," said the prince, "you'll find a rare white cat. She's lively and sweet. I'm sure you'll like her."

The king laughed, "You're a strange fellow, to joke over the right to a throne."

Expecting a cat, the king came forward to open the crystal. The queen, inside, touched a spring that split it open in six parts, like petals. She stood there, like the sun slipping out of clouds, dressed in white and rose silk, a flower crown on her shining locks.

At her amazing beauty, the king cried, "Here is an incomparable princess! Indeed, indeed, she's more than fit to win my crown."

"Majesty," she said modestly, "I've not come to take away your crown. I have six of my own. I beg you, let me give one of them to you, and one to each of your elder sons. I count myself lucky to be able to be related to you by marriage. Your youngest son and I will be content with three kingdoms."

The king and the court and the brothers cheered long and loud for the generosity and charm of the incomparable princess. The three brothers and their ladies were married soon after. For many months to come the court joyously celebrated the alliance of love and royal powers.

Cowlick Ricky

Once there was a queen who had a terribly ugly child. He was a lumpy baby, with a cowlick, and his mother named him Cowlick Ricky. (A cowlick is a tuft of hair that won't lie flat, but sticks up as if a cow had combed it with her tongue.) The queen, his mother, didn't think much of his looks.

But a fairy gave him the gift of being always lovable, extremely intelligent, and witty as well. As an extra gift, he would one day be able to make one other person just as intelligent as he.

The queen felt a little better when she heard of the fairy's gifts. Ricky began to talk at a very young age. He said such amusing things it was fun to have him around. He was good, but never dull. He was funny, kind, and sweet of temper.

A few years later, a neighboring queen had twin girls. The first was lovely, but the queen's joy in her looks was spoiled, for the fortune fairy said she'd be just as stupid as she was beautiful.

Then a second girl was born, so ugly that her mother cried out in alarm. "But," said the fortune fairy, "she'll be so witty and so intelligent, her looks will hardly matter."

"Couldn't you manage to give the first a little wit, and the second a little beauty?" asked the queen.

"No," said the fairy. "The only thing I can do is to give your first, lovely girl the right to make a person she chooses as beautiful as she."

As the girls grew, one became stupider, and the other became uglier. When in company, the bright but ugly sister was more sought after than the pretty one. The pretty one spoke so stupidly she either hurt people's feelings or bored them silly. She was forever knocking things over with her clumsy feet and hands.

One day when she went walking in the woods alone she met a little, crooked young man. He was richly dressed, but very ugly.

It was Cowlick Ricky. He had fallen in love with a portrait of the princess, and had come to have the joy of speaking to so fair a girl. He greeted her with respect and courtesy.

She seemed so sad that he asked, "How is it that one of your great beauty should be unhappy?"

"I don't know," she said stupidly.

"Beauty is so rare a thing," said Ricky. "Nothing but your beauty should matter to you."

"I'd rather be as ugly as you are, and not stupid," said the princess, in her usual heavy way.

"Now I'm sure you're clever," said Ricky. "Only the clever have sense enough to know they know nothing."

"I don't know," said the princess. "I do know I'm hopelessly stupid. And it makes me very unhappy."

"Is stupidity all that troubles you?" he said. "I can soon cure that."

"How?" she asked, open-mouthed.

"I'm Prince Cowlick Ricky," he said. "I have the power to give perfect intelligence to the one I love best. You, Princess, are that best-loved person. I'll give you intelligence, if you'll consent to marry me."

The princess was unable to say a word.

"I see you don't like very much the idea of marrying me," he said. "I understand. But you needn't marry me right away. You may have a year to get used to the idea. I'll give you intelligence right away. You may wait until this time next year to marry me."

The poor girl was so stupid she imagined that anything a year off would never truly happen. So she agreed. But she didn't want to marry Ricky at all.

She gave her promise, and felt her whole mind spin. Suddenly, she could think. She could say witty things, clear things, wise things, endearing things, all in the most appropriate words.

Ricky and she talked for a while. She was bubbling so with wit that he had a hard time keeping up with her. It was a joy to him to talk to her.

The princess returned to the palace. Her quick tongue and clever mind amazed everyone. Now that both her looks and her mind were so extraordinarily good, she quite outshone her younger sister.

Her father, the king, even asked her advice about affairs of state. All the world heard of the change in her. Princes came from far and near to beg her hand in marriage.

Her father said, "Think it over, my clever girl. The throne-room is packed with anxious, first-class princes. Decide for yourself whom you'd best marry."

The princess went walking in the woods, to decide. The more intelligent one is, the more one weighs the reasons for and against doing anything. That's why intelligent folk find it hard to make decisions.

The princess' thoughts were cut short by the sound of many busy voices. One voice said, "Stir up the fire." Another said, "We'll put the tables here." Yet another said, "Where's the gold ladle?"

There in the glen were some thirty chefs, of the special kind who prepare outdoor feasts. Each had a fox tippet nodding over his ear, as a sign of excellence in his profession. Gallon pots, firkins of butter, seasonings, spits, and cooks' tools were laid out in order.

The princess asked what feast they were preparing.

"Highness," they said, "tomorrow is Prince Cowlick Ricky's wedding day. There'll be a forest feast for the court after the ceremony."

She remembered then. It was just a year since she'd promised to wed Prince Ricky. Her new wits had hidden all her earlier stupidity in the back of her head.

Ricky himself appeared a moment later. "Princess, you make me the happiest man alive. I've come to keep my promise. And I suppose you, too, have come to keep yours."

"Frankly, no," said the princess. "To a fool, I might make a kinder answer. But with you, I can only be honest. I'm not used to the idea of marrying you. I don't wish to be used to it. I'm sure I shall never be used to it."

"You amaze me," said Ricky.

"A fool would argue that a princess must keep her promise," said the princess. "But your intelligence is above such vulgar, common thinking. I can reason with you. Remember, a fool made you a promise. But I am no longer that fool, so I'm not bound by the promise made by that fool."

Cowlick Ricky's answer was ready. "Madam, you say that a fool would have the right to insist that you keep your word. Surely a wise man, too, has the right to use that argument when the happiness of his whole life is at stake. For why should the stupid be better off than the wise? Therefore, dearest madam, I do not concede your argument to be true. But now, let's talk concretely. You don't like my ugliness. That's understood. But aside from that, is there anything else about me you don't like? How about my manners, and my family? What about my intelligence or my principles? Do they displease you in any way?"

Said the princess, "In all these ways, you are most lovable."

"If that's true," said Cowlick Ricky, "I hope to be happy. For you can make me a handsome man, if you wish."

"What do you mean?" asked the princess, who had really enjoyed hearing someone who could beat her in an argument.

"I mean this," Ricky said. "As you know, a fairy enabled me to make my beloved intelligent. The same fairy enabled you to make your beloved beautiful."

"If that is true," said the princess, "I wish with all my heart for you to be the handsomest prince in the world. Insofar as I am able, I make you the gift of beauty."

She had no sooner said this than Cowlick Ricky seemed to change before her eyes. She thought him quite the handsomest man she'd ever seen. She promised to marry him as soon as her father would permit.

They returned to the castle, and asked the king's permission to wed. He was delighted to have this noble young man, with a world-wide reputation for goodness and intelligence, as his son-in-law.

They were married the next day. A great and glorious feast was held in the forest, just as clever Cowlick Ricky had foreseen.

The Seven Crow Princes

ONCE there was a man who had seven sons and no daughters. He scarcely dared hope to have a girl. But at last his wife did have another baby, and it was a girl.

All the family rejoiced. The father wanted to baptize the little girl at once. He sent the boys to the river for water. They were good boys, and they hurried to obey. They hurried so much that the boy with the pitcher dropped it into the running water. They splashed about and peered into the water, all seven of them. But the pitcher had disappeared. They didn't know what to do, for they did not dare go home empty-handed.

The father waited and waited, and he became very impatient. He looked at the tiny girl in her cradle. "Drat those boys!" he cried. "What are they up to now? May they all turn into crows!"

Immediately the father heard a sound of wings rushing overhead, and he saw seven black birds fly into the sky.

That was more than he'd expected. He wished he'd been more patient. It was too late now, for he could not undo the curse. The parents were sad to lose their good boys. They gave the best of care to the little girl, to make up for it.

She was a child full of smiles. She grew prettier every day. Her parents did not tell her that because of her the seven brothers had been lost. They did not want her to feel badly.

But one day, she heard a woman say, "She's a nice girl. But just the same, because of her, her seven brothers were lost."

The little girl was horrified. What had she done to her brothers? She asked her parents, and they knew they would have to tell her the truth.

Her father said, "It was no fault of yours. This is what happened." And he told her all he knew.

The little girl grew very sad. Seven fine boys had vanished, just because she'd been born. Night and day she worried, and wondered about her seven brothers.

At last she decided she must roam the world until she found them.

She took only a ring her mother had given her, and a bit of bread. Then she set off.

She walked until she came to the end of the world. Then she went toward the sun. The sun burns terribly as you get close to it. So she changed direction. She went toward the moon. But the moon is cold, and smells of death. Then she went to the stars, and they were very kind.

The morning star gave her a sharp little bone, and said, "You'll need a bone like this to open the glass mountain where your brothers are." The little girl wrapped the bone carefully in her handkerchief, and put it in her pocket.

When she got to the glass mountain, its gates were locked. She took out her handkerchief and untied it. But the pointed bone was gone. It was lost.

How was she to open the door of the glass mountain? She knew that her brothers were inside, and she wanted desperately to free them. But she had no key.

The brave girl decided to make one. She cut off her little finger, sharpened the little bone, and with it she opened the gate of the glass mountain and went in.

Inside was a dwarf, who asked what she wanted.

"I'm looking for my seven brothers," she answered.

"They're my good masters," said the dwarf. "If you'll wait, they'll soon be here. I'm just getting their dinner."

He was setting a table as he talked. There were seven crystal plates and seven glasses. The girl drank a drop from each glass. She ate a crumb from each piece of bread. Then she dropped her mother's ring into the seventh glass.

Presently there was a rush of wings, and a croaking of crows.

The dwarf said, "I hear my masters coming."

The seven crows came in, and looked at their glasses and plates.

One look was enough. "Someone's been eating in my dish, and drinking in my glass. And that someone is a human being," each one said.

Nevertheless they ate and drank well. When the seventh drank his water, he almost choked on the ring at the bottom of his glass.

He took it out, and at once recognized his mother's ring.

All the crow brothers stared at it. "Has our sister come this long, weary way after us?" they asked.

"I wonder, has she broken the spell? Perhaps we can become people again," said the seventh brother. "How I should like to see her!"

Their sister heard them, and she came from behind the door where she'd been hiding.

The moment her brothers saw her, the spell was broken. They became people again. Fine fellows they were, too. They all hugged their little sister, and shook each other's hands.

Then, with hearts full of joy, they set off for home together.

Bluecrest

Once there was a widowed king, rich in land and gold, who had a daughter who was as lovely as the springtime. April was her name. Her dresses were all of flowing silk, embroidered with sprays of jewels. A wreath of fresh flowers held back her shining hair.

When she was fifteen, her father remarried.

The new queen, too, had a daughter, whose godmother was Fairy Fretful. But not even fairy power could make this girl either pretty or pleasant. Her name was Trouty, for her face was speckled like a trout's belly. Her hair was a web of tangles, as greasy as her yellowish skin.

Nevertheless the queen loved Trouty and wanted her to have everything. Envy made her hate the very sight of April, and long to do her harm.

One day, the king said, "Isn't it time we found royal husbands for our girls?"

"Yes," said the queen. "Trouty should wed the greatest prince alive. She's an adorable girl, not vain and silly like April. Of course," she continued slyly, "Trouty's the elder. So April mayn't even think of marrying yet. First we must marry my Trouty to the best man alive."

The king agreed, for he hated quarrels. He left the girls' marriage plans entirely up to the queen.

She quickly invited King Crispin to visit them. He was known far and wide as the richest, kindest, and best of rulers.

Then that sneaky queen bought up every yard of cloth in town. Trouty had sixty-two dresses made, and the rest of the cloth the queen burned. There wasn't a smidgin left for April to buy.

The day King Crispin came, the queen had her servants steal all April's lovely clothes. April had to borrow an old, dirty dress from one of the maids. She was so embarrassed that she hid in a corner when King Crispin arrived.

The queen fussed and fluttered, and flattered the young king. She presented Trouty to him. Trouty was dressed in a blaze of glory, but it made her ugliness more plain.

Crispin tried to ignore Trouty. The queen kept shoving her in front of him.

"Isn't there another princess, named April?" he asked at last.

"There she is," said Trouty, pointing, and giggling rudely. "She's hiding because she looks so sloppy."

April blushed, but the more she blushed the more beautiful she became.

The young king caught his breath. He bowed low, and said, "My lady, beauty as great as yours needs no adornment."

The queen cried crossly, "King Crispin, April's a wickedly vain girl. Compliments make her even worse."

Crispin talked with April for three solid hours. He knew the queen was wild. But he couldn't help himself.

Truthless Trouty and her terrible mother went to the king, and told him that April had insulted their guest. They made him agree to lock her in a tower until Crispin had gone home.

Shut in alone, April wept bitterly. She had liked Crispin so much. She knew her stepmother wanted to keep him away from her.

Crispin could talk only of April. He longed to see her again. The queen ordered everyone to say untrue, hateful things about April. "She hits her maid and kicks her cat," lied one. "She's a miser; that's why she dresses in rags," said another. "She's cross and crazy," lied a third.

Crispin was not deceived by their lies. He could hardly hide his anger. "April is modest, sweet, and fair to see," he said to himself. "I know her heart is modest, sweet, and lovely, too."

Next day Trouty sent Crispin presents. Platoons of servants brought him stacks of books and clothes and boxes full of jewels. "Majesty," said the footman, "these are from the charming princess you met yesterday. She asks you to be her knight."

"Marvelous!" he cried. "How kind of the incomparable Princess April!"

"Pardon, sire, you've mistaken the name," mumbled the footman. "The gifts are from Princess Trouty."

"Trouty?" said the king, coldly. "Then, I regret I cannot accept the honor. A ruler may not involve himself." He sent the presents back at once.

How Trouty and her mother raged!

That night at dinner, Crispin looked in vain for April. Each time a door opened, he turned to see if it were she. At last he asked the queen about her.

"Her father has shut her up in a tower, until after Trouty marries," said the queen.

"Why should he put so perfect a girl in prison?" asked Crispin.

"How do I know?" snapped the queen. "And if I did know, I wouldn't tell you."

Crispin was so enraged that he left the table. He summoned a lord who had accompanied him. "I don't care how you do it," said Crispin, "but, by bribe, by threat, or by begging, get one of April's servants to tell where she is."

The lord had no difficulty in finding a willing servant. He soon returned to the king and told him that he was to be at the tower window at ten that night.

But the servant who had arranged the meeting was the queen's spy. In no time, the queen knew of the plan. She decided to put Trouty in April's place at the window. They rehearsed their plot all afternoon.

It was very dark that night. Crispin had to feel his way toward the window. He had no idea that Trouty had sneaked into April's place. He poured out his heart to the unseen girl at the window. He told Trouty all the things he had wanted to say to April to win her love.

Trouty whispered that she was wretched with her cruel stepmother, and sick of waiting for Trouty to marry. The young king begged her to be his bride. He took off his ring, put it on Trouty's finger, and swore eternal love. He left, but not before Trouty had promised to be at the window again the next night.

The next night it was pitch black. The king summoned a flying chariot, drawn by winged frogs, which had been given him by a kind enchanter friend. Trouty was waiting, heavily veiled. He helped her through the window, and they got into his chariot. Crispin still thought Trouty was April.

"Where shall I take you for our wedding?" he asked.

She answered that she wanted the blessing of her godmother, Fairy Fretful. Off they flew to Fretful's house.

There, Trouty, still veiled, hurried Fretful into a side room. She explained what was going on, and asked her help.

Fretful went right to the king. She said, sternly, "Sire, here's my goddaughter, Princess Trouty. You've sworn eternal love to her. I insist you marry her at once."

Crispin gasped. He was horrified. "What?" he cried. "I, marry this sly, mean, ugly thing? Never! And if she says I promised her anything, she's lying."

Fretful stopped him, angrily. "Mind your manners. You'd better be respectful with me."

"I will give you all respect, Madam Fretful," said Crispin, "if you will give me my true princess."

"Faithless king!" Trouty howled. "I'm your true princess. You put this ring on my finger. You swore you loved me, last night at the tower window."

"I've been tricked," said Crispin. "But I will not be made a fool of into the bargain. Madam, please order my chariot. I must leave, at once."

"No, sire, that's up to me. You go or stay as I choose," replied Fretful. She touched his shoulder, and Crispin found his feet stuck fast to the floor.

"Stone me, skin me alive, if you will. I'll marry no one but April. My mind is made up." Crispin folded his arms, and stood firm.

Fretful howled; she begged; she insisted; she threatened. Trouty whined and whimpered; she capered and cajoled; she screeched, implored, and wept.

Crispin stood firm. Not a word did he say.

This went on for twenty days and twenty nights. No one slept or ate or sat. At last Fretful, worn out, said, "Crispin, you're a fool. Take your choice: either seven years of punishment for your stubbornness or marriage to my godchild, Trouty."

For the first time in twenty days, Crispin spoke. "Do what you will with me. I'll marry no one but April."

"Very well, fool," raged Fretful. "You'll suffer for seven long years. Now, fly away if you want. The window's open."

King Crispin saw he had been changed into a bird. His arms were feathered wings. His body was tiny and covered with bright blue feathers. He had an ivory beak and jewel-bright eyes. A white plume atop his head formed a crown. He had a beautiful, bird-like voice with which to sing and talk.

Quickly he flew from Fretful's mansion.

His one aim was to find April and beg her to wait until his seven years' punishment would end.

Fretful sent Trouty back to the queen. When the queen learned her plot had failed, she stormed against April. "She'll be sorry she took Crispin away from my daughter," she screeched.

She pulled another plot out of her mean imagination. She dressed Trouty up, and put on her head a queen's crown. She led her to April's cell.

"Here's your stepsister," said the queen.

"She's just come from her wedding. She's King Crispin's wife now."

As Trouty held out her hand to poor April, she made King Crispin's ring flash. April recognized that ring. It convinced her that Trouty was really Crispin's queen.

April cried out in despair, "Leave me now. Haven't you done me harm enough already?"

April wept all night at her window, singing her sorrow into the darkness. The next night, too, she wept and sang.

All this time, Bluecrest Crispin had been searching for his love. He had flown all round the palace, sure that April was imprisoned somewhere. But he dared not come too close to the windows, in case Trouty might see him.

Opposite April's tower window was a tall cypress tree. Bluecrest Crispin perched high in its branches to rest. Then he heard a sad voice, lamenting about a lost love.

Bluecrest knew that dearest voice. He sped to April's window. "Fairest princess, don't be sad," he said.

"Who are you?" cried April, startled and bewildered by the sight of the beautiful, speaking bird.

"Princess, I am ready to die of happiness at sight of you," said the strange bird. "Do you not recognize King Crispin? Fairy Fretful has changed me into a bird for seven years. But nothing can change the love I have for you."

"How can it be? Has Crispin, the greatest of kings, come to be this tiny bird?" said the princess.

"This enchantment is the price I paid for my love of you," answered Bluecrest.

"Love?" said April. "If you had loved me, you'd never have married Trouty. I saw your ring on her finger, when she came covered with royal jewels to laugh at me in my prison."

"Trouty says I married her? She lies," said Bluecrest. "They wanted you to think I'd forgotten you. I admit they tricked me into taking Trouty away in my chariot, in your place. But I wasn't fooled for long. I chose to become a helpless bird for seven years, rather than break faith with you."

April realized that Crispin had been true to her. She was so glad to be able to see him again, that she forgot her imprisonment.

At dawn they had to separate, lest they be found out. But they promised to meet every night at the window.

Bluecrest wanted to show April a sign of his love. He flew far and fast to his own castle, and in through an open window. He took a pair of beautiful diamond earrings from his jewel box. That night, he gave them to April.

The next night, Bluecrest brought her a bracelet, cut from a single huge emerald.

The night after that he brought April a watch, made entirely from one big pearl.

Each day he flew to his palace. Each night he brought April another wonderful gift.

Soon April had a marvelous collection. She wore the jewels only at night, to please Bluecrest. During the day she hid them.

Two years went by. April no longer wept over her imprisonment. Time flew, for she spent each night with the one she loved best.

Meanwhile, her mean stepmother was still trying to find a man who would marry Trouty. She sent ambassadors to every court imaginable. But as soon as Trouty's name was mentioned the ambassadors were sent away. The queen decided it must be April's fault. She hated April more than ever.

Late one night, the queen and Trouty went to the tower to question April. Snoopily, the queen bent to listen at the door. She thought she heard a duet being sung, for April had a bird-sweet voice.

"Trouty, she's tricked us," cried the queen, rushing in.

Quick as lightning April shut the window, to give Bluecrest a chance to fly off.

"You're plotting to overthrow the government," screamed the queen. "You're a spy and a traitor!"

"That's impossible," said April. "I've never left this cell. I see no one but the servant you send me."

The queen and Trouty weren't listening. They were staring at April's brilliant jewels.

"Where did you get those jewels?" yelped Trouty. "You're more carefully dressed than the finest lady at court."

"I've nothing to do all day but dress myself, and comb my hair," said April. "It keeps me busy. As for the jewels, I just found them here."

The furious queen dragged Trouty out.

"Let's punish her, horribly," said Trouty.

"No," snarled the queen, "not yet. Maybe she got those jewels from some fairy who is protecting her. Punishing her would only make the fairy kinder. First we must find out what she's up to."

They sent a girl to pretend she was April's maid, and share her cell. But April suspected at once that the girl was a spy. April was heartbroken to miss Bluecrest. She heard him flying about outside, but she dared not open the window, for fear he might be seen and captured.

After a month of spying, the false maid was tired out. She fell into a deep sleep.

April hurried to the window and sang,
"Bluecrest, blue as sky and sea,
Be quick, Bluecrest, and fly to me."

Bluecrest came at once. He and April spent the night rejoicing, and talking happily.

During two more nights, the spy slept deep. Bluecrest and April were overjoyed.

But the next night, the spy was less sleepy. She woke, and lay quiet, listening. The moonlight showed her the princess, talking at the window to a handsome bird.

At dawn the bird flew off. The spy ran to the queen to tell her the news.

Trouty exclaimed, "The bird must be Crispin!"

"How dare they? We'll have our revenge," cried the queen.

The queen told the spy to pretend she'd seen nothing. She sent her back to April's cell.

That night April sang as usual,
"Bluecrest, blue as sky and sea,
Be quick, Bluecrest, and fly to me."
But she sang all night in vain.

The vicious queen had given orders. Every branch of the cypress had been hung with razors and two-edged swords.

When Bluecrest had flown to his cypress tree his feet were cut. He dropped, and his wings were cut. He fell, and he was pierced by a sword. Wounded, he had just managed to drag himself back to his tree. He lay, half-dead, among its leaves.

Bluecrest wanted to die. He was sure that April had betrayed him. He supposed that she had bought her freedom by telling the queen about her nightly visitor.

But Bluecrest Crispin had a faithful friend still. The enchanter, the one who had given him his frog-drawn chariot, had begun a search for Bluecrest two years before. He had gone round the world eight times, without finding the king. Now, on his ninth trip, he came near the wood where Bluecrest lay. The enchanter stopped, and blew his horn, as he had done many times and in many places before.

"King Crispin, where are you?" he called.

The king was roused by the voice of his best friend.

"Come to the tall cypress tree," he called weakly.

The enchanter looked, but saw only a bird.

"I am Bluecrest Crispin now," said the king.

The enchanter gasped, but he quickly recovered and took charge. He bound up the bird's wounds with herbs, and after a few well-chosen magic words, Bluecrest was all but cured.

Bluecrest told his story. He said that he was sure April had betrayed him in order to be freed from prison.

"What a disgusting creature," said the enchanter. "Forget her. If she could betray your love, my lord, she isn't worth loving. I'm afraid I can't change you back to your own shape. But we must think of a plan to keep you safe until I can find out what to do."

"Put me in a cat-proof cage in your house," said the king.

"Yes, sire, but that's not enough. Your kingdom needs you. Your people can't be without a leader for five more years. We will have to find a solution."

Meanwhile, April sang at her window, night and day,

"Bluecrest, blue as sky and sea,
Be quick, Bluecrest, and fly to me."

She didn't care who heard her. She was terribly afraid that Trouty and the queen had hurt the bird. They told her nothing, for they wanted her to suffer the agonies of doubt.

April's father had been ill for some time. When he died the entire kingdom rose up to chase out Trouty and her mother. They had been cruel and proud with everyone. Now they were hated. The queen died of fright, and Trouty escaped to her godmother, Fretful.

The people begged April to be their queen. The lords came to free her, and she was crowned with great rejoicing.

Even as queen, April's one wish was to see Bluecrest again. She straightened out the affairs of state, and appointed a council to rule in her stead for a while. Then she packed up Crispin's marvelous jewel collection, and alone, one dark night, she left to search for her bird king.

All the enchanter's magic had failed to give Bluecrest back his own shape. At last he decided to go and see Fretful, and try to bargain with her, for Crispin's people desperately needed their king. The enchanter proposed his bargain to Fretful: that Crispin was to receive Trouty as a guest for a few months, and Fretful was to change Bluecrest back into Crispin, so that he might try to make up his mind to marry Trouty. Fretful agreed to the bargain.

Fretful dressed Trouty in gold and silver, and sent her to Crispin. He was now in his own shape again. He just couldn't imagine marrying Trouty. The very look of her horrified him. Day after day went by, as his enchanter friend tried to persuade him.

April had disguised herself as a poor peasant. She had come by sea, by horse, by mule—by night, by day, looking for Bluecrest.

One day she came to a brook, and decided to rest there. As she bathed her tired feet, an old lady appeared. "What are you doing, my dear?" asked the old lady.

"I'm looking for Bluecrest," said April, sadly, and she told her story.

In a flash the old lady turned into a bright young fairy. "Lovely April," she said, "my colleague, Fretful, has changed Bluecrest back into King Crispin. He is at his palace. You shall see him, and, if you are brave, you will find a happy ending to your story. Here are four eggs. When you are in real need, break one. It will help you."

April headed for Crispin's kingdom, the eggs wrapped in her kerchief. After seven days and seven nights of walking she came to a mountain that rose straight up, like a tall, tall building. Every time she put her foot on it, she slipped back. At last she thought of the eggs, and she broke one. It held little golden grippers that she slipped over her shoes. With them to hold her, she climbed the mountain. Once at the top, she didn't dare try to go down the other side, for it was just as steep, and she would have fallen to her death. She broke another egg.

Out flew a chariot, drawn by two pigeons. As April looked, the pigeons and the chariot grew until they were the right size to carry her. She got in, and said, "Little birds, I'll be grateful forever if you'll bring me to Crispin's kingdom."

The kindly pigeons carried her night and day, until they came to Crispin's kingdom. April thanked them, and kissed them good-by.

Timid but determined, April dirtied her face with soot so that no one would recognize her. She asked where she could see the king.

"Tomorrow he's going to make a public announcement of his engagement to Princess Trouty, in the cathedral square," she was told.

April's heart sank, then soared with indignation. "Trouty! While I've been worrying about him, he's decided to marry that cruel girl. He's forgotten all we promised."

Nevertheless she went with the crowd to the square the next day.

Trouty soon appeared, gorgeously dressed, and ugly as ever. April came up to her. "Who is the dirty peasant that dares come so close to my excellent person?" Trouty cried.

"I sell precious things," answered April, taking out the emerald bracelet Crispin had given her. It shed a blaze of green fire in the sunlight. Trouty immediately wanted it.

"I'll give you fifty cents for it," said Trouty.

"Show it to experts, my lady. Then we'll set a price," said April.

Trouty, full of self-importance, pranced up to King Crispin. When he saw the bracelet that he had once given April, he was speechless. To hide his emotion, he said quickly, "I had thought there was but one of those in the world. But there must be two. Buy the bracelet."

Trouty went back to April. "Don't dilly-dally. How much?" she snapped.

"All your gold couldn't match its worth," said April. "You may keep it, if I may spend the night in the royal echo chamber."

"Is that all? Very well," laughed Trouty, thinking she'd outwitted a stupid peasant.

It was Crispin who had told April, as they talked at her tower window, all about the royal echo chamber. It was a room right under the king's own bedchamber. Anything said there could be heard in the king's room, and talk in the king's room could be heard in the echo chamber.

That night in the echo chamber, April said to King Crispin, "Have you forgotten? Once I was dear to you. Now Trouty has taken my place."

The servants heard her, but they didn't stop her. They knew that the king would not be disturbed, for he had been taking medicine to make him sleep, every night since he had lost April. Without it, he'd have died of longing and lack of sleep.

April didn't know what to think, when Crispin showed no sign of having heard her. Desperate, she broke one of her eggs.

Inside was a steel and gold carriage, drawn by pink mice, and driven by a gray rat. Four tiny figures, who could dance and do tricks, sat in the carriage.

When Trouty went out for her evening walk, April let the mice trot the carriage across the sidewalk. The dancers stepped out and did their tricks.

Trouty wanted them for herself right away. "How much, peasant?" she snarled.

"Money can't buy them. Let me spend another night in the echo chamber, and I'll give them to you," said April.

"Done," said Trouty.

That night in the echo chamber, April whispered softly every tender, loving thing she could imagine. She reminded the king of their shared happiness. She spoke of her grief without him. But Crispin slept sound, and never heard a word. His sleeping medicine worked well.

April was indignant when she heard that Crispin still intended to wed Trouty. "I'm stupid to love him so, when he doesn't love me," she thought. Still she knew she loved him.

So she broke the fourth egg. It produced a box that held six toy birds. They could sing as if alive; they could tell fortunes; and they knew more about medicine than any doctors.

As April waited outside Trouty's room, a servant came up to her.

"Peasant," he said, "you make a lot of noise at night. It's lucky the king takes medicine to make him sleep sound. Otherwise he'd never have slept a wink, these last two nights."

April understood at last why Crispin had paid no attention to her. She took a handful of jewels from her sack, and said, "If you give the king some sugar-pills tonight, instead of his sleeping medicine, you may have these."

The servant's eyes popped at sight of the jewels. He promised to do as April asked.

Just then, Trouty came by. "What have you this time?" she snapped.

"I have astrologers, singers, and doctors in this box," replied April.

The birds began to sing most delightfully. One bird cocked an eye at Trouty, and said,

"A diet of fresh fruit would clear your com-complexion. You eat too much candy."

"Well!" said Trouty, astonished. "I must have these birds. How much do you want?"

"The same as usual. Let me sleep in the echo chamber tonight," said April.

"Done," said Trouty, and grabbed the box.

Night came. April sat in the echo chamber, and whispered clearly, "I've braved every danger to find you. I've left my comfort, my friends, my people, for your sake. How can you forget me?"

At first, Crispin thought he was dreaming. He couldn't imagine where April might be. He cried, "It's a cruel dream that reminds me of April, who betrayed me to our enemy."

When April heard that, she quickly told him what had really happened.

"But where are you now?" cried Crispin.

"Have you forgotten you told me about the echo chamber?" asked April.

The king rushed down, and pushed open the door. He saw April in her simple gray dress, her hair tumbling over her shoulders. He knelt at her feet, and they wept for joy.

Soon both their stories were told, and no shadow of suspicion darkened their love. Their only worry now was Fairy Fretful. Even as they talked about her, the door opened and in came the enchanter and the fairy who had given April the eggs. They said they would combine their powers to keep Fretful helpless.

Trouty heard that the king had gone to the echo chamber. Always snooping, she went there to spy on him. When she saw April, she almost died of shame and rage.

The enchanter and the fairy turned her into a toad. Croaking, she hopped off into the night.

King Crispin and April were married at once. They were happy beyond telling to be together at last, after so many miseries.

The Royal Ram

THERE once was a king and he had three daughters. They were all beautiful. But the fairest and kindest was the youngest. Her name was Wonder, and she was her father's favorite. To her he gave even more presents than to the others. She always shared them so promptly that no one was jealous of her.

Once, the king had to be away at war for a long time. When the girls heard he'd won the fight at last, they dressed gaily to welcome him home. One wore green, with emerald jewels. Another wore blue, with turquoise jewels. The youngest wore white, with diamonds.

The king arrived and his girls welcomed him with hugs and congratulations. At supper that night he said to the eldest daughter, "Tell me, why did you wear a green dress tonight?"

"Sire," she said, "we heard of your great bravery in battle. I wore green to show my pride and joy at your safe return."

"Well said," smiled the king. "And you, my dear, why did you wear blue?" he asked.

"Sire," she said, "I wore blue to show how we'd begged heaven to keep you safe. Your return is as joyful as blue skies at morning."

"Well said," smiled the king. "And you, Wonder, in your white, why did you choose that dress?"

"Because it makes me look pretty," she said at once.

"Is that all?" said the king, disappointed. He was rather selfish and quick-tempered, and liked to feel that his girls adored him. "Had you no other reason?"

"Father, my reason was only the wish to be as pretty as possible. For the least we, who love you, can do, is to delight your eyes as much as we can."

"A clever answer, indeed!" cried the king. "Now suppose you tell me what you dreamt last night."

The first daughter said she'd dreamed the king gave her a dress all glinting with gold and gems. The second daughter had dreamed that he had brought her a ball-gown, and a golden spindle.

Wonder said, "I dreamed it was my second

130

Adrienne Ségur

sister's wedding day. You, sire, called me, and said, 'Come, I myself will pour water for you to wash your hands!'"

The vain king frowned. He stumped off to bed. "That girl is insolent and proud," he muttered. "She thinks I should be her servant— I, the king!"

Soon he had worked himself into a rage. He called for the captain of the guard, and cried, "You heard Wonder's wicked dream. You see how she plots against me. Take her deep into the forest, and cut her throat. Bring me back her heart and tongue, to prove you've obeyed."

The captain was horrified. But he didn't dare make the king angrier. He promised to do a good job.

He sent for Wonder, saying that her father wanted her.

"His Majesty is in the forest," he said.

It was sunrise as they went out. Wonder saw tears in the captain's eyes.

"Is something wrong? Do tell me. I'd like to try to help," said the kind princess.

"My lady," said the captain, "I've been given a terrible task. Your father has ordered me to kill you."

The princess grew pale. "Have you really the courage to kill me?" she asked. "I've been your friend since I was little. I've done nothing wrong. I've loved and obeyed my father always."

"My lady, I cannot kill you. But I can do no better than to leave you here, alone. I'll go, and convince your father that you're dead."

Wonder thanked the captain, and hurried off. She walked until noon. Bushes tore her dress and scratched her fair skin. She grew tired, and dizzy with hunger.

When she heard a sheep bleat, she stopped. "Maybe I can find a shepherd's family, and exchange this gown for a peasant's dress," she thought. "I'll need a disguise, now that I've been cast out of my home into the world."

She went toward the sound of sheep, and came to a big clearing. There stood a great ram, whiter than snow, golden-horned, flower-garlanded, and decked with jewels. Orange blossoms made a carpet about him. A golden tent shaded him. A hundred sheep and rams, decked with jewels only a little less handsome, stood near. They weren't cropping grass. They were drinking lemonade, and eating iced strawberries and cream. There were two tables of bridge players, and several pairs of sheep were playing chess.

Wonder stared. She looked in vain for a shepherd. When the big ram saw her, he leapt lightly over to her side, and said, "Princess, won't you join us? You've nothing to fear from gentle sheep. Tell me, why have you come?"

"I had to leave home, for my father wanted me killed," replied the princess.

"Stay with us then. You'll be safe here. You'd be most welcome among us," said the amazing ram.

He called for a carriage. Six kids pulled up a huge pumpkin. It had been hollowed out, dried, and decorated. It was big enough to hold two people in its velvet-lined shell.

The lordly ram helped Wonder in, and sat beside her. Rapidly the kids took them to a great rock set into a hill. The ram touched the rock with his hoof, and it rolled back to reveal a cave.

"Don't be alarmed, princess," he said. "Follow me."

They entered the cave and went down a steep slope. Down and down they went, into the depths of a tremendous cavern. It opened out suddenly into a plain of flowers. A river of perfumed water ran sparkling through the plain. There were beautiful fountains of delicious tasting liquid. Stores of food in fantastic designs were set out in imitations of the strangest trees imaginable. There were oaks of hams, and pines of chickens, and maples of cheeses, and copper beeches of lobster. There were flower-like piles, too, of cakes and cookies and jars of jams and syrups. There were hedges made of diamonds and pearls, gold and silver. The air was so pure there that nothing spoiled. All the food stayed just right for eating at any time.

The ram showed Wonder beautiful gardens, rosebushes and honeysuckle twined to make sweet scented tents along the way. Vines had been trained to make rooms where candelabra, mirrors, and fine paintings hung.

"This place is for you, princess," said the ram. "Here you may live in peace. Your every order will be obeyed."

"How kind and how generous you are, Sir Ram," said the princess. "But I admit, I'm rather dazed, and a little frightened, at this strange world of yours. Please take me back to my own world now."

"Don't be frightened," said the ram. "Stay, at least until you hear my story. I am the son of a long line of kings. Once I ruled happily over a large realm, in peace and plenty. I loved to hunt. One day, hunting a stag, I went so fast I left my friends behind. The stag leapt into a lake, and I followed. To my amazement the water wasn't chill, but warm. The lake dried up, and opened into a pit of flames. I was tossed down a cliff into a hole surrounded by fire. There I saw a fairy I'd dreaded for years, a ghastly creature named Ragtag.

" 'What's this all about?' I asked.

" 'You've insulted me too often,' she cried. 'I want revenge. You're going to be one of my sheep, for as long as I please. My sheep are as smart as you, and can talk, too.'

"At a wave of her wand, I found myself here, changed into the ram you see before you. The rest of the flock made me their king. All of them are unlucky people who once displeased

Ragtag, and she turned them into sheep, too.

"Often as I roamed the forest with my flock I saw you, princess, walking with your ladies. I longed to speak to you. But it would have been ridiculous. You would have laughed, if a ram had leapt up and declared his love for you."

Wonder was almost too bewildered to answer. But she agreed to stay in the ram's strange kingdom, and she thanked the ram sincerely for his kindness.

Wonder soon learned that King Ram was both sensible and clever. His conversation was a joy. His love for Wonder was strong and real. She began to appreciate him and to love being with him.

He said that he hoped some day to be free of Ragtag's spell. Then, in his human form and and in his own kingdom, he would try to make her happy. Meanwhile, they lived pleasantly, listening to music, picnicking, talking of all sorts of things.

One day, word came that Wonder's eldest sister was about to marry a great king.

"Oh, how I would love to see her wedding!" said Wonder.

"Why not?" said the ram. "Go when you wish. But please, please promise to come back."

Wonder promised, and the ram sent her to her home splendidly equipped with beautiful clothes and a royal carriage.

When she arrived at her father's palace, everyone wondered who the very lovely, very rich princess might be. The king noticed her, too, and she was afraid that he might recognize her. But he was so sure Wonder had died years before that he suspected nothing.

Nevertheless Wonder was afraid to stay. She left before the ceremony was over.

The king had wanted to meet the unknown lady. He wasn't pleased that she had left before he could speak to her. "Should the unknown princess appear again," he commanded, "shut the palace gates, and send for me. I must know who she is."

During Wonder's short absence the ram king had missed her very much. He welcomed her back with great rejoicing and many wonderful presents.

Not long after, Wonder's second sister was to be married. Wonder again told the ram she would like to attend the wedding. She promised to come back as quickly as she had before.

"I will miss you, too," she said. "I'll hurry back, never fear."

Once again she set out, gorgeously dressed. And once again everyone at court turned to stare at her beauty. The king rejoiced to see her. His servants at once locked all the gates. After the wedding, when Wonder tried to leave, she found every door locked.

The king came to find her. "Don't be alarmed," he said. "I should like you to come to the wedding reception with my other guests."

He led Wonder into the banquet hall. Taking a golden basin and pitcher, he said, "Come, I myself will pour water for you to wash your hands."

With a little cry, Wonder remembered the dream that had begun her troubles. The memory was so strong, she forgot herself, and cried, "You see, father, my dream's come true, and it held no harm at all. It is my sister's wedding day, and you've poured water for me, just as I dreamed."

The king knew then that she was not simply a stranger who reminded him of his lost child.

Overjoyed, he knelt at her feet. "Can you forgive my terrible temper?" he said. "I thought you plotted to remove me from my throne. Now, however, your dream has come true. So let me make amends by setting you on my throne, where I once feared to see you. Your sisters are married to great kings. You, too, shall be a great queen."

He summoned all the court, put his crown upon her head, and cried, "Long live Queen Wonder!" Her sisters hugged her and the whole court beamed with happiness. Wonder laughed and cried together, in the bliss of being loved by her family once more.

At the great banquet she told her story. There were many questions to answer, and many experiences to share.

Meanwhile, the ram waited and waited. The hour of Wonder's expected return had long passed.

"I'm too ugly. She's left forever," he mourned. "I can't live without her. Ragtag, witch-fairy, your revenge on me is too cruel to bear."

When he could stand it no longer, he went to the palace, running wildly all the way. At the gates, he asked to see Wonder. He was rudely refused. He dashed back and forth, distracted, afraid that he had lost his beautiful Wonder forever.

He begged the guards to admit him. They laughed, and turned away. Finally, in a transport of grief, the ram lay down at the gates and died.

Wonder had no idea what had happened. She'd forgotten time in her pleasure at being with her family.

The king suggested they all go for a drive, to see the palace lit up by night in celebration of the wedding. Torches flared everywhere. There was dancing in the streets.

As they left the palace, Wonder chanced to look down. There on the ground near the gates lay the body of her beloved ram.

She ran to his side. When she saw that he would never breathe again, or leap or laugh again, she wept bitterly.

She learned, too, that even the most royal, most lucky persons suffer like everyone else. And sometimes the greatest pains come amid the greatest joys.

Bright, Deardeer, and Kit

KING Kind was a good king. Everyone loved him and his lovely wife, Queen Gentle. They had a little girl, and they called her Bright, for she was such a bright and happy child, and had a shining head of hair.

Soon after Bright was born, her mother died. The king was heartbroken, but he found comfort in his beautiful little daughter.

A year later, the king's council demanded that he find another wife, for the throne needed an heir. At first the king refused. But at last he had to agree, for the good of his country.

He said to his Secretary of State, "Friend, find me a princess who'll be good to my little Bright. It's all I ask of a wife."

King Battle, in the next kingdom, had a daughter, Princess Rigid. She was a pretty girl, and very clever, and the Secretary of State thought that she would make a fine wife for his king. He had no difficulty in getting King Battle's consent to the marriage, for truth to tell, Rigid had a most unpleasant disposition, and her father was glad to be rid of her.

King Kind thought she seemed pleasant enough, and the marriage took place at once.

Bright was now three years old. She was frightened of Rigid's sharp glinting eyes, and her father saw that she was unhappy with her stepmother.

He arranged it so that Bright wouldn't see her often. But when she did see the little girl, Queen Rigid was hard put to hide her dislike

135

A. Séguin

of the delightful and charming little princess.

Soon Rigid had a baby girl of her own, and she called her Dark. Dark was pretty, though less pretty than Bright, and she had some of her mother's mean character. When no one was looking, she'd pinch and bite her stepsister, and break her toys.

Rigid could plainly see that her child wasn't perfect, and that the king's favorite was still Bright, who grew more lovely and sweet-natured each day. It made the queen hate Bright all the more. When Bright was seven, Queen Rigid thought of a wicked plan. Bright had a little cart that was drawn by two ostriches. It was cared for by a young page called Piggo. Now Piggo loved sweets more than anything, and this gave the queen an idea.

She gave Piggo sweets every day. Soon he thought only of candy, and how to get more of it. One day Queen Rigid said, "Piggo, it's up to you. You can earn all the candy you want, for the rest of your life. Or you can disobey me, and never get another piece."

"No more candy? I'd hate that," said Piggo. "What do you want me to do?"

"It's easy. Bring Bright to the forbidden Lilac Forest."

"I can't do that. She'd be enchanted. She'd never come back," said Piggo, who was fond of his little mistress.

"Then, farewell," said Rigid. "You get no more candy, ever."

"Don't say that, Majesty. I couldn't stand it!" cried Piggo.

"Then do as I say. Get Bright into the Lilac Forest."

"What will the king say?" whimpered Piggo.

"I'll take care of him. Lose Bright. Come to me, and I'll send you away safe, with your candies."

With a sigh Piggo agreed. Next day, when Piggo brought Bright her cart, he felt miserable. But he was afraid of Queen Rigid. He turned the cart toward the Lilac Forest, and tried to think of candy all the way.

"What pretty lilacs!" said Bright, at the forest gate. "I'll bring father some."

She jumped down, and crossed over into the enchanted forest.

At once Piggo was sorry. He called, "Come back!"

But Bright was already enchanted. She could no longer see or hear him. The forest closed around her.

She picked lilacs until she was tired and hot. She thought it was time to go home, but she saw nothing but lilac trees. "Piggo," she called. No one answered. She walked and walked and called and called. No one answered.

"What will father think?" she wondered. At last she was tired, so she lay down under the lilacs and slept. It was morning when she woke. A cat was meowing softly. It was a white cat, watching her with kind eyes.

"Why Kit, how handsome you are!" said Bright. "Can you take me to your home? I'm so hungry."

The cat meowed, and pointed with his little paw to a package. Bright opened it. It held four slices of fresh bread and butter. Bright ate hungrily, sharing the meal with the cat. "Thanks for breakfast, Kit," said Bright. "Can you show me where to find help in this forest?"

The cat nodded. He led Bright through the forest until they came to a noble mansion set in a wide, fenced park. Kit went through the fence by a tiny door that was just big enough for him.

Bright waited, and presently the golden doors swung wide to admit her. She went in, and followed Kit through dozens of beautiful rooms. At last they came to a blue and gold room, more beautiful than the rest, where on a couch

of fresh green leaves sat a lovely white deer.

The deer said, "Welcome, Bright. Kit and I are glad to see you. I know your family well."

"Please, my lady, send me to father," said Bright.

"I can't," sighed Deardeer. "You're under the spell of the Lilac Forest Enchanter. Kit and I are, too. All I can do is send dreams to your father, to tell him you're safe with me."

"Shall I never see him again?" cried Bright.

"The future is unknown," said Deardeer. "For now, we'll try to make you happy. Come see your room."

The room was hung with rose silk, and white velvet, and the furniture was of gold. There were two portraits on the wall. One was of a beautiful young woman, the other of a handsome young man. Both of them looked as if they might be of royal birth.

"Who are they, Deardeer?" asked Bright.

"One day you'll know," said Deardeer. "Now, let's have dinner."

Deardeer had a low white satin couch. There was a high stool with a red cushion on it for Kit. Bright sat on an ivory chair, between them. Graceful gazelles waited on them. After dinner they walked in the garden. Bright was very sleepy, and soon went to her room. Gazelles tucked her into bed, and she fell asleep right away.

She slept very deeply. When she awoke, it seemed to her that she'd been asleep for a long, long time. She felt quite different, and she seemed to know many many things.

Yet the room where she lay was just the same as when she had gone to bed.

She went to the mirror. Indeed, she had grown. She was a young lady now. She had to admit she was pretty, with a soft, wise, shy smile. Quickly she dressed, and went to ask what had happened.

"Deardeer," she cried, "last night I was a child. Today, I'm a grown girl."

"Today's your fourteenth birthday, child," said Deardeer. "You've slept a special sleep for seven years. Kit and I wanted to spare you the tiresome part of growing and learning. We've taught you in your sleep. You've learned what an educated woman should know. Come, you'll see."

Deardeer led Bright to her study. Bright ran at once to the piano, and found that she could play very well. She picked up a pen, and wrote beautifully. There were hundreds of books, and she realized that she had read them all. As for her drawing and painting, it was really quite excellent.

She threw her arms around Deardeer's neck.

"What wonderful friends you are!" she said. "No better present was ever given anyone. How can I thank you enough?"

After a while Bright asked, "How is my father?"

"He's well. He's alone now, and thinks often of you. He knows you're safe here, at least."

"Where are Queen Rigid and Dark?" asked Bright.

"Queen Rigid died in a fit of temper," said Deardeer. "Dark has just married Prince Fierce. He'll cure her bad temper, if anyone can."

Time went quickly, for there were so many things to do. Only sometimes did Bright feel lonely, for she had no one to talk to, except Deardeer. And Deardeer she saw only at mealtimes.

Deardeer had made Bright promise to stay inside the park.

"Keep out of that forest," she said, with a shudder.

"I will," said Bright. "But why?"

"It's a terrible place," said Deardeer. She would say no more.

One morning Bright sat at a window, thinking of home. A parrot came and sat on her window sill.

"Good day, Bright," he squeaked. "Lonely, aren't you? I'll come talk to you, if you promise not to tell Deardeer and Kit."

"Why not, pretty Poll?" said Bright.

"If you don't promise not to tell them you've seen me, I'll fly off at once," cried Poll. "They hate me. They're not pretty, and wise, and kind, like you."

"I promise," said Bright. She was delighted to have a new friend, someone to talk to at last. And she was charmed by his pretty compliments.

Poll came each day and told her stories. One day he said, "I have news of your father."

"Is he all right?" exclaimed Bright.

"Yes, but he misses you. He wants me to help you get out of this prison."

"Prison?" said Bright. "Kit and Deardeer are so good to me. This is no prison."

"Ah, you don't know them," said Poll. "They're wickedly clever. They hate me because I know the secret talisman, and I've helped their victims escape."

"What talisman? And why should they keep anyone prisoner?" asked Bright, more and more puzzled.

"They'd die of loneliness without a charming, pretty girl like you to amuse them. As for the talisman, it's just a rose. Pick that rose, and it will free you to go back to your father."

"But there are no roses in these gardens," said Bright.

"I know. I'll tell you tomorrow where the rose grows. Do you doubt me? Just ask Deardeer for a rose. See what she says. Judge for yourself," said Poll, and flew away.

Poll's silly flattery had driven all Bright's gratitude to her friends out of her mind. She

thought only of herself, in a vain, pig-headed way. She believed the words of a parrot who'd never done her any kindness. She went to find Deardeer.

"Why are there no roses in the garden?" Bright asked.

Deardeer shivered, and said, "Bright, even the name of that flower is cursed in this house. It hides a terrible threat."

Deardeer's tone was so troubled that Bright dared ask no more.

When next Poll came to the window, he said, "Was I not right about Deardeer and the rose?" Bright had to admit that he was.

"Come to the forest, then," said Poll. "I'll lead you to where the rose of freedom grows."

"How can I?" said Bright. "Kit walks with me wherever I go."

"Send him off," said Poll. "If he won't go, leave him behind."

So Bright went walking, and Kit came too, though Bright had tried to go without him. Near the forest gate, Bright tried to send Kit away. He wouldn't go. Poll's vain chatter had so excited Bright that she kicked Kit. Kit gave a sad cry, and ran back to the palace.

"Hurry!" squawked Poll, from outside the gate.

"Here I am," said Bright, stepping into the forest.

"Good!" cried Poll. "Follow me."

He led her through tangles and briars. It was hot, and the road was rough and rocky. There were no flowers, and no birds sang.

"Quick, quick," squawked Poll. "Remember your father!"

At last he cried, "Here we are."

At the center of a fenced-in spot stood a rose tree. Atop the tree was one huge rose.

"Pick it, Bright," screamed Poll. "You deserve it. Pick it quickly!"

She reached up and broke off the rose.

It slipped from her fingers and vanished in a burst of horrid laughter. "Thanks, stupid Bright, for letting me out of the prison Deardeer put me in. I'm your evil spirit. You're mine now."

"Haw!" squawked Poll. "I don't need a bird disguise now. I'm the Lilac Forest Enchanter. I hate Deardeer and Kit. You've really ruined them, now. How easy it was to win you over! Haw haw!"

Bright was horrified. She struggled back through the forest toward the mansion. Where it had stood was only a heap of weed-grown ruins.

Bright tried to go in after her friends. A toad called, "Shame on you, terrible girl. You've killed your friends. Get out of here."

Bright fell down, weeping. She wept for a long time. She started to look for a shelter for the night. Then she said, "No, I don't deserve a shelter. I shall stay here. I am a wicked, wicked girl."

A voice called, "Be truly sorry for your faults. You may learn to make up for them."

Bright saw a crow overhead. "I am truly sorry," she said. "But that won't help Deardeer and Kit."

"Be brave, Bright," croaked the crow. "Do your best."

Bright wandered on through the forest. She found some berries to eat. "How kind the earth is," she thought. "It gives food even to me."

"Be brave, Bright. Do your best," piped a tree toad.

She made a shelter under some bushes, and there she stayed, day after day.

Weeks sped by. Bright lived in her shelter, and ate the fruit of the forest. She wept for her cruelty, for her lost friends, and for her father. She tried to be brave, and do her best.

One day a huge turtle waddled slowly toward her. "If you'll do as I say, I'll take you out of the forest," said the turtle, in her wrinkly old voice.

"I don't deserve help," said Bright. "My cruelty killed my best friends."

"Are you sure they're dead?" asked the turtle.

"May I hope they're alive?" cried Bright.

"I mayn't speak of that," said the turtle, slowly. "If you're brave enough to get on my back . . . if you're patient enough to stay there six long months . . . if you're obedient enough to not say one single word all that time . . . you'll find out."

"I'd do anything to hear of my friends," said Bright.

"Are you sure? You must be patient. You must say not a single word," said the turtle.

"Please, dear turtle, let's go now, at once. I promise to do my best," said Bright.

For one hundred and eighty days Bright stayed on the turtle's back. She tried to be patient, as the slow turtle crept along, inch by inch. She didn't ask a single question, nor say a single word. She saw a mansion just ahead. It was like Deardeer's ruined home. Bright could have run to it in no time. But she sat silent and still.

At last the turtle stopped at its gates, and said, "Now you may get down from my back. Go into the mansion. Ask for Fairy Goodness. Your obedience and patience will be rewarded."

A lovely girl answered Bright's knock.

"Please, may I see Fairy Goodness?" asked Bright.

"Come with me," the girl said.

They went to a room where sat a beautiful lady. She smiled, and asked, "What do you wish, child?"

"Please, can you tell me of my friends, Deardeer and Kit?" begged Bright.

The lady nodded sadly. She held out a key, and said, "This opens the tall cupboard by the window. See for yourself."

Trembling, Bright opened the cupboard door wide. Inside were stretched the skins of Deardeer and Kit. Bright gave one piercing cry and fell into a swoon.

A handsome young man ran to her side. "The punishment was too harsh, Mother," he whispered.

"It was harsh," said Fairy Goodness. "But nothing else could free her from the Lilac Forest Enchanter."

She touched Bright with her wand, and the girl sat up. "I'll never see my friends again," she said, weeping.

"You're wrong, dear," said the fairy. "You see them now. I am Deardeer. This is my son, Prince Kit. We're glad you're here."

Bright was beside herself with joy.

Fairy Goodness said, "I've told your father to expect you. We'll drive you home."

All three of them got into a pearl-and-gold chariot, and drove to King Kind's palace. The king and all his court were waiting. They cheered as the chariot drove up. The king hugged Bright long and tenderly. Then he thanked Fairy Goodness and her son for all their help.

They celebrated Bright's homecoming for a week. When it was time for Fairy Goodness and her son to depart, Kit and Bright were heartbroken. Then the king had a fine idea. He and Fairy Goodness were married, in a magnificent double ceremony, at the same time as Bright and Kit.

Dark and her husband, Prince Fierce, came often to visit the happy couples. As Dark became sweeter, Fierce became calmer. Soon they, too, were a happy pair.

Bright had little girls who looked like her, and little boys who looked like Kit. They loved each other and all the world, and all the world loved them.

Dawn, the Golden Haired

ONCE upon a time there was a king's daughter who had long, shimmering hair. It was as long as she was tall. She wore it loose about her, like a cape of spun gold, crowned with flowers. Because of the way her golden hair caught the light, she was called Dawn, the Golden Haired. To see her was to love her.

A neighboring king heard of the beauty of Dawn. He felt strongly drawn to her. He sent her an ambassador with many gifts, and letters that begged her to be his bride. He was sure she'd say yes, for he was both young and powerful.

His ambassador was presented to Dawn. She was more particular than the king had supposed, and besides, she'd got out of the wrong side of the bed that day. She made up her mind fast. "No, thank you," she said to the ambassador, without one moment's hesitation.

With wise good manners she sent back the rich gifts. She kept only a packet of English needles, as she didn't want to hurt the king's feelings.

The ambassador returned to the king, who was furiously disappointed with the news. Even the company of his best friend, Welcome, didn't cheer him up. And Welcome was a very cheerful, handsome, agreeable man.

Welcome loved his king. He worried when he saw him so upset. One day he said, "If I'd been the king's ambassador, I'd have come back with Princess Dawn."

A jealous lord told the king. He said, "Sire, Welcome needs to be put in his place. He's too bold. He claims that if he'd seen Princess Dawn he'd have won her heart. He dares to think he's more charming than Your Majesty."

The king was still upset by the princess' refusal. His best friend's boldness was the last straw. He cried, "Throw Welcome in jail. He'll pay for his pride. Let him die of hunger."

Welcome had no food for days. Every evening he crawled to the foot of the jail tower. There he drank a little water from the rain spout. The fifth evening, he sighed, "My king is hard on me. I'm his most loyal subject.

How could I insult him? I love him more than my own life."

The king was passing by, and listened. The jealous courtier tried to call him away. But he sent for Welcome.

Welcome said, "Sire, why are you angry with me? Even death in prison is nothing compared to losing your friendship."

"You set yourself above me," said the king.

"Never," said Welcome. "I said that if I'd been your ambassador to Princess Dawn, she'd have come back here. It's true. For I know and love your great goodness. I'd have convinced her of her luck in finding so perfect a husband."

The king said, "I pardon you. Come with me, friend Welcome."

They dined together. Afterwards, the king said, "Welcome, I love Dawn still. Go to her as my ambassador. Perhaps you can convince her."

"I'll go tomorrow," said Welcome.

"But you'll need a large retinue," said the king.

"No, sire," said Welcome. "I need only a good horse, and letters from you."

Early the next day Welcome left, alone, without fuss. As he rode, he thought of how to convince Dawn that she should marry his king. When he had a good idea, he stopped and wrote it down.

One morning he stopped to write near a broad stream. As he was admiring the pretty countryside, he saw a fish out of water. It lay, gleaming and gasping, in the grass. It was a carp, and she might have made him a good dinner. But he felt sorry for her. Gently, he put her back in the water.

She leapt, and spun, and turned to him, saying, "Welcome, thank you. You've saved my life. I hope to return the favor one day."

The next day, Welcome was riding along when he saw a crow being chased by a huge eagle. "Why should the big always beat the small?" he thought. He took his bow and arrow, and shot the eagle dead.

The crow flew by, and said, "Thank you, Welcome. You've saved my life. I hope to return the favor one day."

Welcome admired the crow's courtesy, and rode on. Early next morning, he found an owl caught in a net.

"Why must men torment birds and beasts and other men?" he thought. He set the owl free.

The owl swirled above his head, and hooted, "Thank you, Welcome. You saved my life. I hope to return the favor one day."

The next day found him at the palace of Dawn, the Golden Haired. It was worthy of its princess. "It won't be easy to make Dawn leave such a fine kingdom," Welcome thought.

He stopped at an inn to bathe himself and dress in court clothes. Then he set off for the castle, accompanied by a smart little dog he'd bought as a gift for Dawn.

Guards announced him to Princess Dawn. "He has a pleasant name," said she. "I wager he's agreeable."

"He is, Your Highness," said her maid. "I peeked out the window. And he's very handsome."

"You shouldn't peek," laughed Dawn. "But what's done is done. Admit this Welcome. And get fresh flowers for my hair. Give me the blue satin gown, my high heels, and my French fan. Send a sweeper to polish up the throne. I don't want to be a disappointment to the ambassador."

Her maids scurried and flurried and hurried. Dawn was soon ready for her visitor.

For several moments Welcome stood awed by her beauty. Then bravely he took heart and began to plead for his king.

When he had finished, Dawn said, "Welcome, the reasons you've given me for marrying your king are interesting and sensible. I've enjoyed hearing you. But I've something else on my mind. I lost a ring by the river last month. I can think of nothing else until it's found."

Welcome thought, "The princess forgets that rings are less important than kings." But he wasn't discouraged. He offered Dawn the lively little dog. She said, "Thank you. But I can't even receive gifts until I get back my ring."

The dog was a merry, clever little fellow called Tailspin. When they were alone, and Tailspin saw Welcome puzzling over what to do next, he said, "Don't fret. If the ring's to be found, you'll find it."

The next morning, as they were walking, Tailspin led Welcome's steps closer to the river. They were soon near to its bank. Welcome started with surprise as someone called his name.

He looked around, but he saw no one. Tailspin, who had short legs and was nearer to the water, peered down and said, "Strike me blue! There's a big shiny carp calling you!"

"Yes, Welcome, it is I," said the carp. "Now I can repay you for saving my life. Here's the ring."

Welcome knelt, and took the princess' ring from the carp's mouth. He thanked her heartily, then set off straightway for the palace.

Dawn, the Golden Haired, heard that he wanted to see her. "I suppose he wants to say good-by, poor man," she thought. "I asked him to do the impossible."

Welcome came before her smiling, and said, "Madam, here's your ring. Now, what do you think about marrying my king?"

Dazed, Dawn took the ring. She said, "Some kind fairy must have helped you."

"No, I know no fairies," said Welcome. "But I had a great desire to succeed."

"Since you have such a good will," she said, "I'll ask for another favor. Unless you can do it, I'll never marry. Prince Grue, my neighbor, wants to marry me. He's a horrid giant, tall as a tower, who eats men the way monkeys eat bananas. He's been killing my citizens because I won't marry him. If you want me to think about marriage, you must bring me his head."

Welcome took a deep breath and said, "I'll try. I'll surely be beaten and eaten. But I'll die fighting."

The princess said she'd help him organize a big expedition. But he refused her offer, and set off at once, with Tailspin in his pocket. Every time he asked the way to Grue's castle, people shuddered and said, "Grue is invincible." He felt more and more frightened.

Tailspin cheered him. "Don't worry," he said. "I have a plan. I'll nip his ankles, and when he bends over after me, you whack his head off, one, two, three!"

Welcome patted his brave companion. But he had no hope. The road to Grue's castle was thick with skeletons from Grue's picnic lunches.

Suddenly Grue appeared, so tall that his head rose above the trees. He was singing a bloodthirsty song in a terrible voice, and Welcome at once began to sing, too, in a squawky imitation of Grue. Then he shouted some insults. Grue stopped, and peered down from his great height. When he saw Welcome, he yanked out his club and made ready to squash Welcome flat.

Then out of the sky darted a crow and jabbed Grue in the eyes. He fell dead, and Welcome cut off the giant's head.

"I am glad I could repay you for saving my life," called the crow.

Welcome called back, "Thank you, friend

Adrienne Ségur

crow!" Then he took Grue's horrid head, and set off for Dawn's palace. A thousand citizens followed him, shouting his praises. The princess heard them, and came to meet him.

"Princess Dawn," said Welcome, "your foe is dead. May I present his head? Now will you think about marrying my king?"

"I shall," she answered. "But first, bring me a bottle of water from Gloom Cave. It's deep in a glen near here. Fire-eating dragons guard a pit full of poisonous snakes and spiders. At the bottom of the pit is a little cave. In the cave is the fountain of health and beauty. Its water makes loveliness lovely forever. It makes the ugly beautiful. It keeps the young young, and makes the old young again. You can see, Welcome, that I'd never leave my kingdom without taking some of this useful water."

"Madam, you're lovely now. You need no magic water," said the patient Welcome. "But you seem to feel that my dying would amuse you. So I'll go, though it means death."

Welcome and Tailspin went off toward the dreadful glen. Everyone who saw them said, "What a pity for this young man to die so horribly. Where does our princess get her wild ideas?"

Within sight of Gloom Cave they sat down to rest. Ahead of them was a big rock. From behind it reared a roaring dragon, fire blazing from his eyes and mouth. Tailspin shivered with fright and wanted only to disappear. But Welcome bravely made ready to die in the service of his king. He drew his sword. Then he took the bottle that the princess had given him, and showed it to Tailspin.

"Little friend," he said, "my end is near. When the dragons have done with my dead body, fill this bottle with my blood and bring it to the princess. Then go to my king and tell him my story."

As he spoke, he heard his name called.

"Who's that?" he cried.

In the crook of an old tree was an owl.

"It is I," said the owl. "Now I can repay you for saving my life. Bring the wicker basket that holds the bottle, and put it around my neck. I'll get you the magic water."

"How will you do it, and come out alive?" said Welcome.

"No one ever notices me in there. I know the place well," said the owl.

Filled with gratitude, Welcome tied the bottle round the owl's neck, and the owl flew off. In ten minutes he was back. The bottle was full, and carefully corked. Welcome thanked the owl heartily.

Then he went happily back to the palace, and gave the bottle to Dawn, the Golden Haired.

She thanked him, and said, "You're a very charming young man. If you had asked, I'd have married you."

Welcome blushed. "It's true you're more beautiful to my eyes than the very light of day. But I must be faithful to my king."

The king married Dawn soon afterward, amid great rejoicing. The king was happy at first. But Dawn talked so often of Welcome's courage and loyalty that he grew displeased. Finally jealous courtiers said to the king, "How do you stand it? Your queen loves Welcome, not you. She thinks he's more of a man than you are. He carried out the tasks that made her accept your proposal."

"I've noticed she does talk about him often," said the ungrateful king. "I'll have him thrown in jail."

So once again Welcome was jailed. When Dawn heard of it she begged the king to remember his services, and set him free. But it did no good at all, because the more she begged, the more jealous did the king become.

One day a thought came to the king. "Perhaps I'm not handsome enough. What if I rub my face with her magic water?"

Now Dawn had kept the bottle on the mantel, where she could look at it often. One day a maid had knocked it down when she was dusting, and the bottle was smashed to pieces. She swept them up and hid them so no one would scold her, then she looked around for something to replace the bottle. She remembered seeing a similar bottle in the king's room. She got it, and put it on the mantel in place of the magic water. The maid didn't know what was in the king's bottle. It was full of a poison that the king used to kill great lords when they had committed great crimes. Instead of cutting off their heads, the executioner rubbed their faces with liquid from the bottle. It made them fall asleep at once and die.

The king, of course, thought the bottle on the mantel was full of magic beauty water. He rubbed his face with it. At once he fell asleep, and died.

When Tailspin heard the news, he ran immediately to the queen and whispered, "Majesty, don't forget your loyal servant, Welcome."

The queen hadn't forgotten him. She set him free with her own hands. Then she placed a gold crown on his head, and a royal cloak on his shoulders.

She said, "Come, Welcome. I make you my king."

They were married at once. Everyone was glad to have so good, brave, and wise a king. Their reign was long, happy, and a blessing to the country.

Finn, the Keen Falcon

A FARMER and his wife had three daughters. The two older girls could think of nothing but fancy clothes and pretty trinkets. But the youngest, who was the prettiest, worked happily on the farm, and never complained.

The farmer went to town every week to market his produce, and to buy things for his family.

One market day, he said, "Girls, what shall I buy you?"

"Satin for a new dress," cried the eldest.

"For me too," said the second.

The youngest said softly, "I'd like a scarlet flower."

Her sisters giggled. "But the fields are full of flowers," they said.

She said again, more softly, "I'd like a scarlet flower."

In town that day the farmer quickly found satin for dresses. Then he looked everywhere for a scarlet flower. There was none to be had.

The others mocked their young sister while they sewed their new gowns, and the father looked on with a worried frown. But the young girl said only, "Never mind, father. Next time."

Next market day the farmer said, "Girls, what shall I buy you?"

"A lace hanky," said the eldest.

"For me too," said the second.

The third girl said, "I'd like a scarlet flower." Her voice was so quiet and serious that her sisters could think of nothing to say.

The farmer bought the two lace handkerchiefs, then looked for a scarlet flower. No scarlet flowers were for sale. He wanted his girls to be happy. He loved his youngest best, though he tried not to show it. She was as helpful as the others were selfish. He was sorry to disappoint her again.

On the way home he saw a man holding a scarlet flower in his right hand.

"How much is that flower?" he asked.

"You may have the flower, gladly, if you'll let your youngest daughter marry Finn, the Keen Falcon," said the man.

The farmer hesitated. He didn't know Finn, the Keen Falcon. A falcon is a wild, proud bird. What did it mean?

He thought, "If she doesn't like this Finn, she can refuse him herself." He decided to take the scarlet flower.

When he got home, he gave the older girls their hankies.

"Here's your scarlet flower," he said to the youngest girl. "But don't take it, unless you want to be engaged to Finn, the Keen Falcon. If you don't like him, refuse him."

"Oh, I do like him," she said quietly, and smiled.

"What? Have you met him?" asked the farmer.

"Yes," she said. "Finn is a prince who can change into a falcon. He's very good and kind. I've seen him often at church, and he says he loves me."

After supper she went to her room and laid the scarlet flower on the window sill. She sat dreaming. Soon a black speck showed in the sunset sky. It came closer, until she saw it was a falcon. His silent flight brought him to the sill. As he stepped into the room, he became a young man.

They talked quietly together. Finn the Keen loved the girl who had chosen the scarlet flower. As he was leaving, he gave her a long feather from his wing.

"Whenever you want anything," he said, "go outside, and wave this feather to the right, thinking of what you want. Good-by until tomorrow, dear heart."

Each night that week, Finn the Keen came to visit.

Then it was Sunday. The older girls got into their new dresses and perfumed their lace hankies. They were proud of their fine clothes, and they came to tease their young sister.

"We're going to church," they said. "You can get dressed up, too, in your cow-milking gown. With your scarlet flower, you'll look grand," they teased.

The youngest girl merely smiled and waved good-by from the doorway.

When they had gone she went outside. She waved the falcon's feather to the right, and thought of the things she wanted. Immediately, her braids changed to curls, her cotton dress changed to satin, wonderfully embroidered in gold and diamonds, and a magnificent carriage drew up. She got in and drove to church. Everyone tried to get a close look at her after the service. She was so beautiful and so magnificently dressed that they thought she must be a great princess who was traveling through their village.

But she hurried off as soon as the service was over. She got home just before her family and waved her feather to the left. At once all the finery vanished and she set about cooking the dinner as if nothing had happened.

Her sisters could hardly eat, they were so dazed by the beautiful princess they'd seen.

The same thing happened three Sundays in a row. The fourth time, the youngest girl was rolling pie crust when her sisters came home.

One of them saw a diamond pin tangled in her hair. She nudged the other sister and pointed to the pin.

The youngest girl wondered why they were suddenly so quiet. She found the pin, and rolled it quietly into a piece of pie dough, and put the lump of dough into her pocket.

But it was too late! The older girls had become suspicious. They spied on her all day. That evening, they saw the falcon glide in to their sister's window. They heard the loving voice of Finn the Keen.

They were furiously jealous—green with envy, and red with anger. They weren't going to let their little sister marry ahead of them, not they!

Next evening they hung sharp knives, razors, and scythes in the trees and around their sister's window sill.

The youngest girl put the scarlet flower on the sill. The falcon sped through the sky. When he neared the window, he was stabbed and slashed by the sharp blades.

Finn the Keen cried a terrible cry. He believed his love had tried to kill him. "Wretch," he cried, "before you see me again, you'll break three iron staves. Before you see me again, you'll wear out three pairs of iron shoes. Before you see me again, you'll eat three loaves of iron bread."

Then he disappeared.

The girl was broken-hearted. She waved the magic feather, wishing that she might find Finn and care for his wounds. But the feather's power had vanished.

She made up her mind to find Finn. An ironmonger made her three iron staves, three pairs of iron shoes, and three loaves of iron bread. With these she set out.

Over wide plains she went, over high mountains, and across wild forests. She broke an iron staff. She wore out a pair of iron shoes. She sucked on a loaf of iron bread until it was small as a pill. On and on she went.

She came to a hut that stood on chicken-legs. "Please, pretty hut, may I come in? I'm so tired, I don't know what to do."

The door opened. "Who are you?" asked the old woman sitting by the fire.

The girl told her story to the old woman, who was a powerful sorceress. "You'll have to hurry," said the old woman, "for Finn is engaged to marry a princess. Here's a ball of wool. Go wherever it goes. Here are a gold spindle and a spinning wheel. Set them up when you get to the sea's edge, and they will spin a gold thread. The princess will come by and want to buy them. Say no. Say she may have them if you may see Finn, the Keen Falcon.

"Now go. The ball will lead you to my sister."

The girl followed the ball through storms and snow and sun. She broke a second staff. She wore out a second pair of iron shoes. She ate a second loaf of iron bread.

At last the ball stopped before another hut on chicken legs. An old woman stuck her head out and cried, "Who are you?"

The girl told her story again.

"Hurry, hurry," screeched the woman. "Finn the Keen is getting married soon. Here's a silver dish and a golden egg. At the sea's edge take them out. Finn's princess will come by and want to buy them. Say no. Say she may have them if you may see Finn, the Keen Falcon. Now, be off to see my sister."

The girl put the dish and the egg into her bundle, and ran after the ball again. She crossed a vast desert, she climbed a huge mountain. She broke the third iron staff. She wore out the third pair of iron shoes. She ate the third loaf of iron bread.

Adrienne Ségur

At last the ball stopped before another hut on chicken legs. A third old woman stood at the door. "You've come a long way," she shouted. "It's almost too late. Finn will marry in three days. Take this embroidery hoop and needle. It embroiders all by itself. At the sea's edge take it out. Finn's princess will want to buy it. Say no. Say she may have it, if you may see Finn, the Keen Falcon. Now, hurry, hurry."

Up and down dizzying hills went the ball, over swamps and sand dunes and lonely beaches. At last it stopped at the sea's edge, on a beach near a castle.

The girl sat down at last. She took out the golden spindle and wheel, and the golden thread began to spin off.

Finn's princess came by and saw the spinning wheel at work. "I want that," she said. "How much is it?"

"It's not for sale, my lady. You may have it if I may see Finn, the Keen Falcon."

The princess thought for a moment, then she smiled. She had a magic hairpin that made its wearer fall fast asleep. She would put it in Finn's hair. Then she needn't care what girl came to see him.

"Good," she said. She took the spindle.

The girl saw Finn, but he was asleep. She whispered her story into his ear. But he slept on.

Next day she rolled the golden egg in the silver dish. The princess came by.

"I want that!" she cried. "How much?"

"You may have it, if I may see Finn, the Keen Falcon," said the girl.

Once again the princess put Finn to sleep. When the girl knelt by the sleeping prince, she told him how she'd longed to see him, and how she had worn out three iron staves, three pairs of iron shoes, and three loaves of iron. But he slept on.

Next day was Finn's wedding eve. The girl went to the beach. She took out the magic hoop and needle and they began to embroider all by themselves.

The princess saw them and said, "I want those. How much?"

"You may have them, if I may see Finn, the Keen Falcon," said the girl.

Once again she found him asleep. Heartbroken, she bid him good-by. She ran her fingers through his hair in a last farewell.

When her fingers touched the magic pin, she drew it out. Finn, the Keen Falcon, awoke and sat up. He saw before him the girl he had loved so much. He smiled, as if in a dream, for while sleeping he'd dreamed she came to him.

When he heard how bravely she'd come to him, he sent his silly princess back to her family.

He ordered a general rejoicing throughout his lands, and the wedding feast went on for three days and three nights. And that is how the youngest sister became the bride of Finn, the Keen Falcon.

Fairies

Once there was a widow who had two girls. The oldest was just like her mother, who was spiteful and mean. The younger girl was generous and gentle, as her father had been, and she was perfectly beautiful as well.

Like likes like they say, and the mother loved the older girl dearly. She hated the younger, who did the housework and cooking for the three of them.

Twice a day the younger girl went to the well for water. She walked a mile each way, carrying a heavy jugful each time.

One day at the well a poor old woman asked her for a drink. "With pleasure, ma'am," she said, and smiled prettily. She rinsed out her pitcher, and filled it with clear water. Then she held the heavy pitcher as the old woman drank.

The woman thanked her. She said, "Because you're helpful and gentle, I will give you a gift. Every time you speak, a precious jewel or a beautiful flower will spring from your lips."

Then she vanished. She was a fairy who had come to test the girl's good heart.

With her pitcher full, the girl went home. Her mother scolded her for being so long at the fountain. "I'm sorry, mother," said the girl. As she spoke, two roses, two pearls, and two diamonds fell from her lips.

"What's that?" screeched the mother. "Where do they come from?"

The girl was both obedient and truthful. She explained what had happened. In the telling, she spread a carpet of diamonds and flowers about her.

"That stupid fairy made a mistake," said her mother. "Fairy gifts are too good for a loon like you. They should have been given to your clever big sister. Next time, she will go after the water."

That afternoon the mother said to her elder girl, "You'll fetch the water today."

"I will not," shouted the mean girl.

"You will too," shouted her mean mother.

She finally went. But she left the big pitcher at home. Instead she carried a tiny silver creamer. At the well was a lady in beautiful clothes. The lady asked for a drink.

"I'm no servant," said the rude girl. "This is

155

my pitcher, not yours. Get your own drink, if you're thirsty."

"Very well," said the lady, who was the fairy in a new disguise. "I'll give you a gift to suit your manners. Every time you speak, a toad or a snake will slither from your mouth."

Her mother was waiting for the girl to return. When she saw her, she cried, "Well, daughter?"

"Well, mother?" shouted the rude girl. Two toads and a snake squirmed from her mouth.

"What's that?" cried her mother. When she heard what had happened, she flew into a fury.

"It's your fault," she screamed at the younger girl. Then she chased her out with a broom.

The poor girl ran into the forest to hide. The king's son was coming home from hunting. He saw the beautiful girl leaning against a tree trunk and weeping. He stopped, and said,

"What's wrong, my dear? Why do you weep?"

"My mother has put me out," she said. At each word, pearls and diamonds fell from her lips and blazed in the grass at her feet.

"What a marvelous thing," exclaimed the king's son. "Do tell me why this happens."

She told him about the fairy at the well. As he listened, he fell in love with her beauty and her good heart. He led her home to his palace. They were married, and reigned happily for years and years and years.

As for her older sister, she grew nastier every day. Even her mother couldn't abide her, especially since she filled the house with slippy, sloppy, slithering things whenever she spoke. At last she left her mother's house, and wandered up and down the world, alone. No one would have anything to do with her, ever.